MW00744913

Steve Hamilton, two-time Edgar Award winning crime fiction writer and bestselling author of the Alex McKnight crime fiction series, to include A Cold Day in Paradise and Misery Bay. "Where did you learn to do this? Because I'll tell you something, sir, you have a natural rhythm in your writing that really pleases the ear. It's something that you can't teach, frankly, and most people who try to write a book just don't have it."

Sue Harrison, award-winning bestselling author of the Mother Earth Father Sky Wood Carver trilogy and the My Brother the Wind Storyteller trilogy. "Chuck, I could tell from your first sentence that you are a good writer. You have a very good voice that fits the characters and the situation. You are a very visual writer. You do amazing stuff with action scenes. You have a gift, Sue.

Eric Gadzinski, award-winning Michigan poet. Author of 'Tattoo'. "I find your novel authentic and, as you write, beautiful and ugly."

Dan Darnarski, award-winning bestselling author of Twenty-One Days in Africa. A book rated along with Hemmingway's Green Hills of Africa and O'Rourke's The Horn of Africa as one of the best books on African big game hunting. "I liked reading it. It read good. It's a great story."

LOVE BURIES A SPRING BIRD

a novel by
Charles Forgrave

LOVE BURIES A SPRING BIRD

For more information contact Charles Forgrave
cforgraveus@yahoo.com

ISBN (Print Edition): 978-1-54392-249-3
ISBN (eBook Edition): 978-1-54392-250-9

Bookbaby
7905 N Crescent Blvd   .
Pennsauken, NJ 08110

Printed in the United States of America.

*This book is for
Linda, Trey and Tishella.*

"You're a spring bird, Jackie. You're just starting out in life.
You still have a lot to learn about being a woman,"
Bunny in conversation with her daughter.

BOOK ONE

The Way We Met

CHAPTER 1

WE SAT TOO FAR BACK IN THE YARD TO SEE THE END OF the village because of the tavern in our way. But Bill saw them both as they came out from behind it and said something to me about it. They both wore swimsuits and walked barefoot and were all white arms and legs and blue and green mauve bathing suits, and as we watched them, they took long careful steps reaching out with their long legs to get off the hot blacktop and swinging their long arms in rhythm to keep their balance and not fall. Then one stepped on a hot tarry spot and then the loose stone chips and got down on her hands and feet and spider walked over to the shoulder of the road, where her friend began picking them off."

"Now's your chance to meet her," Bill said. "Get up off your ass, and get it out there and help her."

"Why don't you?"

"She looks your age. Get up out of that chair, and get out there."

"You get out there."

"Don't you worry one bit. She's a good-looking girl. I'd be out there right now, if she looked a little older. As it is I might go out there anyway." He grinned at me and nodded his head up and down as if he was saying yes to himself.

They were still sitting there.

"Get up off your ass and get it out there," he said. He jabbed his thumb in their direction. "Don't be a chicken shit about it. Just walk out there and introduce yourself."

I felt like he had me on the spot. Like it was now or never as to whether I was a chicken shit. I blushed at the idea of going out but I wanted to really bad.

"You silly ass, what are you afraid of? Get out of that chair and get out there. You'll find things to talk about once you start talking to them. Don't make such a big deal of it."

Now I was mad at him. I decided to show him that I wasn't afraid. I got up out of my chair and started out, walking right up to them.

They both looked up at me.

"Hi, you got some stones stuck to your foot?"

"Yeah, I did. Ouch," she said.

"Do you need some help getting them off?"

"No, Ellie's got them all off now."

"Here, Ellie," she said, "take my hand and help me up."

Ellie helped her up and they started walking again. I thought about saying something to them about not stepping on the hot tarry spots. But I figured it could wait until later.

"Mind if I walk along with you?" I said instead.

"No, not at all."

"Are you staying out here somewhere?"

"Yeah we're staying down at the Fishery."

"Oh, you are? How long have you been there?"

"Since a week ago last Friday."

"Oh, that long? It's funny that I haven't seen you around before this?"

"Well, it's not actually funny. Not if you knew my mom, it's not. We're lucky to go anywhere by ourselves. What about you, where do you live?"

"See that house over there, the one with the big roof. I live in it."

They both looked over at it.

"What are your names?" I said.

"I'm Ellie."

"And, I'm Jackie."

"I'm Cortney," I said. "It's good to meet you both."

"It's good to meet you, too," they both said.

They were looking all about us now and when they thought that they could get away with it, sneaking in a glance at me. I was being careful to talk with them both and not just to one. I sensed that they both wanted me to like them and I didn't want to hurt either of their feelings. I was sizing up their rear ends and when I could get away with it, sneaking in a glance at their boobs. They both looked really good in their bathing suits. But Jackie looked the best. She had all the right curves in all the right places. She was a little shy, but it was a nice kind of shy. We didn't have to walk far before I realized that I liked her best. They both realized it, too. Ellie acted a little hurt by it at first but she soon got over it.

Jackie liked me too and we were nervous now because of it.

"It's really nice out, eh?" I said.

"Yeah, it is."

"Have you guys been swimming?"

"Yeah, we went in for a while this morning."

"Ellie, don't you mean to say, that I went in for a while?"

"Go ahead, Jackie, keep it up and you'll get it."

She made a fist and held it up to her.

"You're acting like a spoiled brat," Jackie said. She jumped away when Ellie poked her arm. She glanced over at me as she did. Her dignity was hurt as well as her arm. I didn't know what to do and I decided to stay out of it. It was between the two of them I figured and probably didn't mean a thing anyway.

"Was the water warm when you went in?"

"No, actually it was like ice."

"What time did you go?"

"It was before lunch. But actually I didn't go in either. The water was too cold. All I did was wade around in it for a while."

"It usually doesn't warm up until later, after the sun's overhead."

"Oh uh-huh, that makes sense."

She smiled at me.

"Next month it'll be cold all day. It's usually so cold by September that everybody quits swimming."

"By then we won't be here."

"Yeah, we'll be back in school."

"Yeah, you both will be, won't you?" I said.

Then we none of us said anything. They looked like they were thinking of something to say. But neither said a word. It was an awkward silence like you always worried about happening when you're off alone for the first time with somebody you liked. I looked up at the sky and not a cloud was in sight anywhere.

"Who are you guys out here with?"

"We're out here with her mom and dad, and her little brother."

"Really?"

"Yeah."

"So you have a little brother, eh Jackie?"

"Yeah I do."

"How old is he?"

"He's five."

"Hey, that's really neat."

"Yikes, it's not neat when it's my brother Willis."

"Ha, ha, he's that bad, eh?"

"Actually, he's that bad and worse."

"Wait until you meet him," Ellie said, "you'll see for yourself."

Hey, I thought, I will be glad to meet her little brother.

"Ellie, how old are you?"

"She's fifteen."

"Thank you, Jackie, but I can answer for myself. I'm fifteen. So big deal, eh Jackie, so you're a whole year older than I am; big whoop?"

Ellie made a fist and poked her arm again. This time Jackie bumped into me as she jumped away.

"Ellie, I can't help it if I'm older than you," she said, her dignity hurt again too.

"Oh, so you can't, eh?"

"No, I can't and you know it too."

"Oh, I do, do I?"

"Yes, you do. So stop acting silly, okay? I'm sorry if I teased you too much, okay?" She said this straight out hoping to put an end to it.

Now Ellie's dignity was hurt, too.

She looked off away from us.

"Did you graduate, Cortney?"

"Yeah I did. A year ago," I said.

She didn't say anything.

We stopped at the driveway into the cabins. We looked in at them and in between them at the lake. I thought that I shouldn't go any further with them. We knew each other's names and I thought that it was enough for now. I felt it was time for me to say goodbye to them and to start back up the road. We would likely see more of each other later. Besides, it was nerve wracking getting as far as I had with them and I felt like being alone for a while.

We were still standing there.

"Well, I guess I'd better get back. My cousin Bill's waiting for me." I pointed back of myself up the road. They both looked at me as if they were waiting for me to say something else. "I'll bring my swimsuit back with me and we can go swimming, together, if you guys want to."

They both smiled now.

"What time should I come back?"

"Whenever you want to."

"I'll come back in a couple hours, then."

"Sure."

"I'll see you both later."

"Yeah, okay."

"Bye then."

"Bye."

"Bye," I said to Ellie.

Ellie said goodbye to me and we turned and walked away. I walked back up the blacktop toward home and they walked in on the gravel driveway toward their cabin. After a short while I looked back and they both were looking back at me. Wow, did I feel good now. Jackie liked me and was everything that I ever wanted in a girl; her white skin, her pretty face, her mauve bathing suit that fit her body like a glove; everything about her. I couldn't wait to get back and see Bill and tell him about her.

CHAPTER 2

I GOT BACK TO THE YARD AND BILL WASN'T THERE. I WENT into the house and no one was in it, either. There was a note on the table. My mom went to town with my Aunt Margaret. It was her grocery shopping day. I sat down on the couch and I looked down at the splotch of sunlight at my feet. I thought about meeting the girls and, feeling good about it, I let myself drift off a little. I snapped back out of it and I walked over next door to see Bill. I knocked on the door and he hollered for me to come in. I opened it and I went in. He was sitting in the living room watching a football game with a friend of his.

They both looked out at me.

"Hey, Cortney, come on in."

I walked in.

"Well, how about it? Did you get acquainted with them, alright?"

"Yeah, I did. We walked all the way down to Gearheart's, together. I know their names now and everything. We're going swimming together, later."

"Well, good. See there was nothing to it? All you did was walk out there and introduce yourself and start talking to them. Woody, this here is my cousin, Cortney. He lives next door."

Woody and I said hello. I sat down on the couch by him. I began to watch the football game but I quit and got back up.

"I think I'll head out?"

They both looked at me.

"Cortney, sit back down," Bill said, "and watch the rest of the game with us. You don't have to rush away."

I thought that I would. But then I decided not to, again.

"No, I guess not? I don't feel like sitting still all that long. I came over to tell you about the girls. I'll talk to you again later, okay?"

"Yeah, okay Cortney. We'll talk to you again later."

Woody and I said goodbye. I walked back out to the door. I went out it and I walked across his yard into ours. I looked up the driveway and my Aunt Margaret's car was parked at the head of it, now. My mom was standing behind it.

"Come on over here," she said, "and get an armful of these groceries."

She leaned into the trunk and she filled up her arms with them. As I walked over to it she started for the house. I leaned into it and I filled up my arms with them and started for the house, too. She held the door open for me and I walked through it and went on into the kitchen. She followed me into it and she knelt down at the refrigerator and put packages of meat into the freezer.

"Sit yours down there on the table," she said.

I sat them down where she told me. My sister Mary walked in from the living room. She knelt down beside her and she took the packages out of the bags and handed them to her. I squeezed in between them to get up to the counter.

My Mom looked up at me.

"Cortney, what are you doing?"

"I'm going to make a sandwich."

"Well, can't it wait until later? When I'm done here I'm going to put something on for all of us?"

"Yeah, it could. But I'm in a hurry."

"Well, what's so important that it can't wait until after we eat, together? After all, we are a family."

I didn't say anything.

I didn't think it was any of her business.

I opened a loaf of bread and I took out a slice. I put a slice of ham and cheese and tomato on it. I added pickles and lettuce and mayo to it. I put a slice of bread on the top of it and I wrapped it up in a napkin and headed for the door. I snatched my swimsuit off the clothesline on my way out to the road.

Iroquois Beach sits in a cedar swamp on Lake Superior. My Great Uncle Victor bought a forty-acre parcel here about a hundred years ago. He built his cabin down on the high sandy land along the water. He built his crib dock out front of it with his twine shed on it. He kept his fish tug tied up to it. But all that's been washed away by the lake. The only thing left is the big pile of rocks that we swim off. My Uncle Victor sold out to our relatives later in life. He kept only the log cabin and a few acres of the land for himself. Lumbering was giving out up in the Dollar Settlement by then. The saw mill was closing down and moving out on the railroad. Everybody was moving down to Iroquois Beach to fish for a living. Fifteen homes were built on Great Uncle Victor's original forty acres before it was over.

Our house sits on a high sandy ridge that runs across the property. Across the blacktop from us a gravel road runs down to the beach where my dad keeps his fish tug pulled up onto the long skids. The Gearheart Fishery is a quarter mile down the road. The ditches to either side of it have brown swamp water in them. You get down there and you look up into the driveway and you see the cabins and, off to the side a little, the fishery buildings, themselves. The cabins are painted a pleasant-looking yellow. The lake behind them is a pleasant summer blue. You look in at them and it's like you're looking at a picture of a resort that you'd see on a tourist brochure.

They were outside standing in a clump of birch trees when I got down there. As I walked in the driveway they both looked out at me. I walked as casually as I could to look cool.

Ellie said hello.

"Hi, Cortney."

"Hi, Ellie. How are you?"

"Good," she said.

We both smiled.

I looked at Jackie. "Hi, Jackie."

"Hi," she said, and smiled, too.

"What are you guys up to?"

"Actually, we're not up to anything?"

"Not anything at all?"

"Well, not absolutely, not anything? Actually, we've been standing here talking."

"We watched you walk in. We think you walk like Justin Bieber."

I held up my swimsuit.

"I brought my swimsuit back with me. Do you guys still want to go swimming?"

"Yeah, we do," said Jackie. "Or, at least I still do?"

She looked at Ellie.

"Jackie, you know that I can't go in, yet?"

She made a face at her and Jackie made one back.

Myself, I didn't know what was going on. Or what to think? I didn't know the first thing about a girl's period.

I thought of another question to ask.

"Does your little brother like to go swimming?"

"Yeah, he does. But he only goes out to his knees."

"Oh, that's too bad."

"Yeah, it is."

It got quiet again.

I thought of another question to ask.

"Please Jackie, can I come out, now?"

We looked at the cabin.

"No, Willis, you can't come out, now. I said for you to stay in there, and I meant it."

"Jackie, I will be good. I promise you I will."

"No, Willis, you won't be good. I don't want you out here with us, okay?"

"My God, Jackie," said a woman from inside. "He said that he would be good? Why wouldn't he? He wants to go outside with you? Let him go out? What's he going to hurt. He's not going to hurt anything, that's what? Besides, he's driving me crazy in here."

He opened the door.

"Walk out right out there, Willis," she said.

As he walked out, she went inside.

"Willis," Jackie said, "if you're not good, I'm taking you back inside."

He didn't say anything.

"This is my brother, Willis," she said.

"Hi, Willis, it's good to meet you."

He didn't say anything to me, either.

"Willis," she said, "Cortney said 'hi' to you. Say 'hi, to him, now."

He ignored her, too.

"It's okay if he doesn't," I said.

"Whoopee, whooper, whoops."

"Willis, stop doing that. I hate it when you do that."

"Whoopee, whooper, whoops."

"Willis, I said for you to stop doing that. If you don't stop it, I'm hollering for Dad and he's going to come out and give you a good hard spanking."

But when she didn't holler for him and he did it again she raised her hand and she ran after him as if she was going to slap him with it. He ran back into the cabin.

"You get back in there and you stay in there."

The woman came back out to the door. She stood behind him with her hands onto her waist and stared out at us.

"Willis is acting-up out here again, Mom. Will you please make him go back inside with you?"

Instead, she went back inside herself. Jackie walked back over to the clump of birch trees to be with us, again. She looked to be upset about everything, now.

CHAPTER 3

"ONE OF THESE DAYS I'M GOING TO MURDER HIM. Whenever there's company over and you want him to behave himself, he acts up like that."

"Jackie, he's still a little boy."

"Well, he doesn't have to act, like that?"

"He's not even five, yet."

"Ellie, you don't have to be around him all the time like I do. He gets on your nerves after a while."

"Yeah, okay, you're right. I know he does."

"Well, there's something wrong with him. I keep telling you that and you never believe me."

"Oh, Jackie, I do, too."

"No, I'm sorry, Ellie, but you don't."

"Okay, so maybe there is something wrong with him, eh; but who can really know about some things, eh?"

She glanced at me and Jackie saw her.

"Ellie," she said, "you never agree with me about anything. So, I don't know why I should expect you to, now? But do a favor for me, will you? Knock off with the eh, eh, stuff? Eh, eh, yourself?"

"Jackie, I just now agreed with you, didn't I? At least I thought that I did? I said that you could be right?"

"Well okay, Ellie, so you did? But it's like I've told you a thousand times before; he's got something wrong with him. He needs to see a doctor."

"Well, if that's the case, why hasn't he?"

"Whoopee, whooper, whoops."

Willis was back out at the door, again.

"Speak of the devil?"

"Yeah, that's for sure?"

"Mom, Willis is back out here, again. Will you please come back out and make him go back inside with you?"

Her mother came back out and she stood behind him and put her hands onto her waist. She stared out at us, like before.

"Oh my God, Jackie, he's a little boy? What is it that you can't understand about that? Will you please leave him alone and let him play!"

She went back inside, herself, instead, again.

Jackie and Ellie hunched their shoulders. They smiled at me and I hunched mine and smiled back.

"Oh my," Ellie said, smiling her crazy grin, "but aren't we lucky. We have Willis in our lives?"

"Ellie," Jackie said, "I'm not talking silly about anything, today, okay? I'm tired of talking silly all the time. Besides, there's nothing happening that I can't handle. And, there's nothing upsetting me, okay? So, can we please talk like ordinary people do, today?"

It got quiet, again.

I thought of another question to ask.

"How did you find this place way out here?"

"We didn't find it, her dad did."

"Well, how did he find it, then?"

"He came out here for a ride and he saw the sign out at the road, and he drove in and asked them about it."

"Was that last winter?"

"Yeah, it was? How did you know that?"

"That's only when it's open?"

They both smiled at me.

I thought of another question to ask.

"How long are you guys staying out here?"

"Two weeks," said Jackie.

"Your dad was lucky to find them," I said. "These cabins sit in here empty all year. Other than you guys and my grandpa nobody else rents them. He stays in them a couple weeks every summer and visits with us."

"Yeah, her dad was lucky to find them," Ellie said. "He reminds us of it all the time, too. The way he goes on about it, you'd think he was Christopher Columbus."

"Well, Ellie, he's proud he found them. If you found them, you would be too. Besides he can't afford to stay out here at a resort."

"Oh my, but can't Daddy's little girl be so protective?"

Oh no, I thought, here we go, again.

"Ellie, think what you want to about it, okay? But I'm not going to fight with you about anything, today. I'm tired of fighting with you about everything under the sun. Besides, no matter what any of us thinks about it, we all love it out here."

"Well, it's usually hot and sticky in town this time of year. At least out here there's usually a cool breeze off the lake."

Wow, they're actually agreeing about something, I thought? Now, what was going on?

"I wish we lived out here."

"Yeah, I wish we did, too."

"Well, we don't. But maybe someday we will?"

"Yeah, we could, someday? Nowadays people can end up living almost, anywhere."

"Yeah, they can. We might end up living up in Canada, somewhere. Maybe even up in the Arctic Circle?"

"Yeah, we might. But who wants to live up there, eh?"

"Yeah, that's for sure. Nobody that I know does."

"I'd rather we lived out here by the lake. Where it's not so cold."

"Yeah, me, too. Maybe our folks will move out here. If they do, we can move out with them."

"Jackie, why wait for them to do it? Why not move out here, ourselves?"

"Well, if you want to move out here, Ellie, go ahead and move. Do it tomorrow, if you want. It's your life? Do as you please with it?"

Ellie said nothing.

It got quiet, again.

In the summer 'downstate people' come 'up north' by the thousands. They stay at a motel for a week or two and they end up falling in love with the place and wanting to stay and live up here.

But they don't know the first thing about our winters. They think that they're as nice as our summers. But I tell them that they're not. That they will never really get to know what it's like to live up here until they come back up in February when it's thirty below out and there's a cold north wind blowing off Lake Superior and they can't see their hands in front of their faces because of the blowing snow. It's a one liner that I like. It brings them back to their senses about the place. True, the air is fresh up here. You can breathe better in it. True, the north woods go on, forever. But, it's like I tell them, too: they will never really get to know what it's like to live up here until they come back up in February and stay for a week or two.

Both Jackie and Ellie on the other hand were born and raised up here. They haven't been fooled by the summers into thinking that the place is a paradise. But they haven't lived out by the lake in the winter, before, either. They've always lived in town where it's not as cold. Myself, I go in to town and I look at the cars out driving in the streets and at the people out walking on the sidewalks, and at all the nice restaurants to eat in, and the place looks like a paradise to me. If the opportunity ever came along, I would move to town in an instant.

"It's amazing how we all feel so different about things, eh? I love the summer's out here. But in the winter, I always wish that I lived in town," I said.

They both looked at me like I didn't know what I was talking about.

"Myself, I think that the warm summers make up for the cold winters. If the opportunity ever came along, I'd move out here in an instant," Ellie said.

"I've never been out here in the wintertime. So, I don't know what they're really like. But if they're as nice as the summers, then l would move out here in an instant, too," Jackie said.

We none of us said anything else.

"How far away are those mountains?"

She pointed out across the lake at them.

"I think they're about thirty miles."

"Wow, I didn't realize they were that far?"

"I had no idea they were that far. They look blue, don't they? But they're actually green," Jackie said, twirling her finger upward. "Science class! We're looking at them through the summer haze."

Both Ellie and I smiled.

"Have you ever been over there?"

"No, I haven't."

"I haven't been right over there. But I've been up in Canada."

"I've been across the river to Soo, Canada. My grandparents on my mother's side live over there."

"I haven't even been over there," I said. "I haven't been anywhere in Canada."

"You haven't, really?"

"Yeah, really?"

"The people are a lot different acting," Jackie said. "They're more sophisticated, or something."

"Yeah, I think they are, too," Ellie said.

CHAPTER 4

THE SUN WAS DOWN BEHIND THE TREES. IT CAME IN AT A slant through them. There was a splotch of it on the ground. We watched it stretch and fade and then disappear, altogether. It began to cool down.

Her mother brought out a plate of sandwiches to us.

She held them out to Ellie.

"Thank you, Bunny."

She held them out to Jackie.

"Mom, what kind are they?"

"Jackie, they're tuna fish? Can't you tell?"

"Ah, Mom, not tuna fish, again?"

"Jackie, will you please stop?"

Jackie took one. Bunny held them out to me.

I took one, too. "Thank you, Bunny."

"Mom, this is Cortney. He lives out here."

"Cortney, it's nice to meet you."

"It's nice to meet you, too."

We both nodded, and smiled.

I waited for Jackie to introduce her, now.

"Jackie, aren't you going to introduce me?"

"Mom, you're standing next to him. Introduce yourself?"

"My God, Jackie, is that what we taught you. No, it's not, girl. We taught you to use your manners and be polite to people?"

"Cortney, that's my mother, Bunny."

"Bunny, it's good to meet you."

We both nodded, and smiled, now, too.

"There, now each of you have a sandwich. I'm taking the rest of these back inside where the bugs can't get at them." Gnats were flying in and out of our faces. "Jackie, when somebody wants another one, you come in and get it for them. Okay?"

"Yeah, okay, Mom."

"Now, at least, Jackie, you can't say that I don't feed you."
She smirked as she went back inside.

Jackie's face turned red.

"Yuck," she said, "just the thought of eating this makes me sick to my stomach."

She held it out at arm's length.

"Jackie, your mother's totally crazy?"

"Not crazy, Ellie, insane. She's been totally insane all her life."

"Shush, the doors' open. She'll hear you."

"So, let her hear me. What is she going to do, come out here and kill me?"

They both giggled. They covered their mouths and they hunched their shoulders and pulled their heads down between them. Neither of them looked to be so brave, now.

"Well, she can kill you, if she wants to. But she's not killing me."

"I'd as soon be dead as have her for my mother, anyway."

They both giggled and covered their mouths, again.

"Jackie," I said, "what are you guys giggling so hard about?"

"Oh, it's my Mom. She's totally insane? Yesterday we asked her real nice-like to buy lunch meat for us, to make sandwiches...."

"...yeah, and you would have thought that she would have gone out, and done it? But, oh no, not her. Not her mother. She went out and she came back with more tuna. Now is that insane, or what?"

She held her sandwich out at arm's length, too.

"Yeah, and if we say anything at all to her, she gets really mad at us. She screams and hollers at us and she calls us names, and raves about how unappreciative we are. You'd think that we did something wrong."

"I think she's brain-dead...?"

"...if she even has a brain?"

They giggled, again.

"Shush, the door's still open."

"So, who cares? I'd as soon be dead as have her as my mother, anyway."

"Jackie, you always act so brave?"

"Ellie, I do not? Why did you say that to me?"

"Because it's true."

"Well okay? So, what if I do? Maybe I'm not perfect, eh? Maybe it's the way I deal with things, okay? Did you even think of that?"

"No, I didn't. And no, it's not okay. I'm tired of your mother calling me names. I don't like her swearing at me, either. Cover your mouth, again. Or she's going to hear you."

Jackie covered her mouth.

"Take a deep breath, and hold it?"

She took a deep breath, and held it.

"Close your eyes and look up at the sky, and don't move."

She did as Ellie asked her to.

I butted in.

"Ellie, what are you doing?"

"Cortney, it'd take the rest of my life to explain it."

Suddenly Jackie stopped her giggling.

"Ellie, what did you do?"

"I helped her stop her giggling."

I raised my eyebrows. We smiled at each other. Well, at least we're ready to go on and talk about something else, now, I thought. I could finally quit worrying about Bunny getting her hands on them, too.

I folded my arms to keep warm.

"Cortney, your arms are trembling."

They reached out and touched them.

I touched them, myself, now. "Wow, are they ever."

Ellie held hers out for us to touch. Jackie and I both touched them. They were trembling as hard as mine.

"I should go home, and let you guys go in?"

"No, I'm okay," said Jackie.

"But, it's freezing out here."

"No, we're okay?" Ellie said.

I didn't say anything.

Actually I didn't want to go home; but when I thought about how warm it would be there and sitting in my favorite chair watching a football game with a bowl of popcorn in my hands, I wasn't so sure about it.

"Jackie," I said, "what's your mother really like? Other than crazy about tuna fish?"

Her face flushed a little.

"Well, she's quiet most of the time. At least she is when she's not drinking. Actually she says very little to you unless she is drinking. But once she is, then watch out. She goes on about all kinds of things. She says that we're all nothing but specks of dust in the cosmos. That our lives here are meaningless. And, if you don't stay there and listen to her, she screams and yells and calls you names. Dad, he gets up and he walks out on her, and leaves her there."

"Yeah" Ellie said. "And, that's when things can get really scary. As in dishes flying and breaking against the wall, scary?"

"Oh wow, for real?

"Yeah, for real," she said. "She scares Willis out of his wits. He cries, and she gets still crazier and throws things even harder."

I didn't say anything.

"She's gone totally insane!"

"What's your Mom really like, Cortney?"

"What do you mean, really like?"

"Well, like Jackie told you. Is she crazy, or nice, or what?"

"Well, she's nice when I'm around her. But I'm not around her that much, to really know?"

"Well, if you don't know what your mother's really like. What's your dad really like?"

"Actually, I'm around him even less?"

"Why are you around him less?"

"Because he works away from home, and he doesn't get back that often."

Neither of them said anything.

"Burr," said Ellie, "I can't stay out here any longer. It's gotten too cold out here for me. I'm going in where it's warm."

She strode off to the cabin.

"Tell Mom that I'll be right in. Okay, Ellie?"

"Yeah, okay, Jackie," she said.

It was dark out and I couldn't see my hand in front of my face. I reached out to touch her to see where she was, and she took it and held it. I guess she thought that's what I wanted her to do. It wasn't. But it was easy to move over to her tree and to stand by her on it, now. She moved over on it to make more room for me.

Now that our shoulders were touching even the cold was bearable.

"Can I come down and see you tomorrow?"

"Yeah, sure?"

"What time should I?"

"Whenever you want to?"

"What time do you get up?"

"I'm usually up by eight."

"Okay, I'll come down about eight, then. I'll bring my boat back and we can go for a ride out to the island, if you want to?"

"Yeah, I do. It sounds fun."

"Good. I'll see you in the morning."

"Yeah, okay," she said.

She squeezed my hand and she let it go. She went inside, and I struck off for home.

CHAPTER 5

THE SKY WAS OVER CAST AND IT WAS PITCH-BLACK DARK
out and I couldn't see the stars. I didn't know if I should walk the
road or the beach back home. If I walked the road back home, I
wouldn't see the opening of it through the trees ahead. I would
have to hold my hands out front of me in case I bumped into a
bear. If I walked the beach back home, I would see the ships out
in the shipping lanes. I would know that there were people out on
them and I wouldn't feel as alone. I decided to walk the beach back
home. The thousand-footers haul crushed coal down to the big city
power plants. My cousin Charlie Horse comes up in the summers
and he stays' down the road at my Grandma and Grandpa's. One
night when he was walking the beach back home he looked out
into the shipping lanes and saw what he thought was a used car lot.
He looked away from it and then back at it and it was still there.
Later when he told Granma and Grandpa about it, they told him
that it was a thousand-foot ship. Later when they told me about it
I laughed so hard that I almost peed my pants. In the daytime, you
can see the white water curling up off their bows and back of them
on the Canadian shoreline, the white dots of summer cottages.
Tonight, a strong wind was blowing in off the lake. It was pushing
the waves up the slope of the beach to the bank. There was no place
left to walk above them and keep your shoes dry. When that happens to me, I walk down through them and I walk along the water. I
still get my shoes wet down there; but the sand is hard and it's easy
to walk. I tripped twice over the driftwood before I got back home.

I've been everywhere around here looking for the best view.
I've been back to the little swamp lakes in along the bluff. I've been
down the road back of the old Jesuit Mission up onto the Spectacle
Lake Overlook. But wherever I've been, I've always thought that
this beach was the best view. I come down here and I walk along it
and I can see every which way for miles. My Great Uncle Dan, he

comes down here and he walks along it, too. He always ends up feeling better about things whenever he does. We like to get him started on telling his stories. He points out into the lake and he says that when he was a kid the shore was out there. He wants us to think of him as a wise old Indian man. But we tease him about his stories, anyway. We tell him that they sound as old as the old Jesuit Mission, itself, and maybe Jesus Christ, himself. It gets him all riled up. His best story is about the Iroquois war party's attack on our village. Our people killed them off to the last man, except for one. They let him live to carry the story of the battle back to his people. They cut off the heads of the others. They stuck them up on poles along the beach to warn off others. People around here think that my Great Uncle Dan is crazy. They want nothing to do with him or his stores. But I love my Great Uncle Dan. I think that he's his own Great Spirit. I come down here to this beach and I have nothing to do with his Great Spirit, or anybody else's, or their sweat lodges or talking circles or any of the other stuff that they preach to us about, or any of their Christian churches, either, and I walk along it and I sort out whatever's bothering me and it never fails me and I always end up feeling good.

I remember some things like they happened to me, yesterday: I turn up the slope of the beach and I walk up through the deepening sand with my shoes sinking down into it and I go through the driftwood scattered there and up past where my dad keeps his boat pulled up onto the long skids and I climb the bank and walk up the beach road looking at the picture window glowing in the dark ahead. I cross the blacktop and I jump the ditch and walk through the yard and up to the door and in.

Dolores looks up at me.

"Hi, Cortney."

"Hi, Delores. How are you?"

"I'm okay, thank you."

We neither of us smiles. I'm surprised to see her there. She watches me as I walk through the living room. She doesn't say anything else to me and I don't say anything else to her, either.

My sister Mary is there, too.

"Hello, Mary."

"Hi, Cortney."

My Mom is also there.

"Hi, Mom."

"Hello, stranger."

I smile at her wise remark. I climb the stairs up to my bedroom and I throw myself down across my bed and I stretch out as big as I can and lie as still as I can and think about Delores. I wonder why she is over visiting. I haven't seen her since I left for Detroit. I don't care to see her now, either. She was the reason that I went off in the first place. I wanted to get away from her. She said that she loved me when actually she didn't love anybody. I said that I loved her when actually I didn't love anybody, either. The lying about it is what got to me. A reaction set in and I ended up feeling sick at myself. But wait, let me back up: I told her that I loved her so I could mess around with her. I found a job for myself but I got lonely and I quit and came back. Now I'm lying here on my bed thinking about Delores in a lot of different ways and wondering why she is over visiting and I'm thinking about Jackie in as many other ways and wondering what she's doing down at the cabin, and waiting for sleep to overtake me.

It isn't much fun.

CHAPTER 6

I WAKE UP IN THE MORNING AND THE SUN IS SHINING IN
my bedroom window. There is a beam of it crossing above my head.
There are dust particles in it. I wave my hand through them and as I
watch it, they swirl around it. I listen for noises downstairs. I don't
hear any and I get up and go down into the living room. I look out
the picture window and it's so bright outside that I squint to see
anywhere. I pull on my trousers and I walk out into the driveway.
I want to see if last night's wind blew the sandy spot into little
waves. It did. It looks like the lake did last night. I cross the lawn
to the edge of the yard and I take a leak into the trees. I walk back
across to the house and I go back inside and look at the clock. It's
eight o'clock. I still have an hour to wait before I can walk down the
road and see Jackie. I cook myself a breakfast of bacon and eggs and
toast. I sit down at the table and I eat it and get back up. I brew a
cup of coffee for myself and I take it back outside with me. I drink
it as Daryl Loonsfoot comes out of his house carrying his lunch box
under his arm. He gets into his truck and he drives off. We wave as
he drives by. I cross the blacktop and I walk down the beach road. I
bail my dad's boat of rainwater and I check the outboard for gas and
start to walk up the lake. I want to see if last night's wind dammed
up the drainage ditch up in Sweet's Bay. It gets dammed up and it
stays dammed up for weeks at a time. Or until another storm comes
along and washes it back out. Or until somebody like myself comes
along and digs it back out. As I walk up the beach I imagine myself
digging a trench across it with the heels of my shoes. I stand, and
I watch as the water runs down through it and washes the dam
back out. But when I get up there the drainage ditch is still flowing.
Disappointed, I turn around and I walk back down the beach to my
boat. I get into it and I take an oar and push it out to where I can
start the outboard. I start it and I speed off down the lake shore
and, out front of the fishery I come hard around. I run back in to

the beach and I land on it and I jump out and run up to the bank. I climb it and I run up the path through the trees to the cabin. I get there, and Willis runs out to meet me. He stops right in front of me and I trip and fall over him. I get back up, and help him back up. He steps back, and looks up at me.

"I saw you coming, I saw you coming."

"Hey, Willis. Thanks for coming out to meet me."

"I saw you coming, I saw you coming."

"Yeah, Willis, you sure did. You did a good job of it, too. Thank you, Willis, for doing that for me. Where's Jackie at? Do you know?"

"Jackie's in the cabin, Jackie's in the cabin."

"Thank you, Willis. Thank you, for telling me that."

"I came out to tell you, I came out to tell you."

He claps his hands and he jumps up and down.

"Well, how about it, eh? Let's you and I go and see her?"

"Here I am," she says, coming out. She raises her arms and she lets them fall. "Willis, he knows that I'm here. Please get out of his way and let him come."

"Hi, Jackie."

"Hi, how are you, today?"

Willis runs back into the cabin.

"Please ignore him, okay?"

"Yeah, okay. He's a riot, sometimes, eh?"

"Yeah, he sure is."

"Hoodoo, hoodoo, hoodoo."

He was inside the screen door, now. His lips were pressed hard against it. They looked like flattened mushrooms.

"Willis, will you please stop doing that? Mom, Willis is out here acting up, again. Will you please come out and make him go back inside with you?"

"Hoodoo, hoodoo, hoodoo."

Her mother came out. She stood behind him and she put her hands onto her waist and stared out at us, like before.

"My God, Jackie, he's a little boy. Leave him alone and let him play. He's not hurting anything."

She turned around and she went back inside.

"Hoodoo, hoodoo, hoodoo."

"Let's walk down to the beach," Jackie said.

We started to walk down through the trees to the beach, together. Halfway down to it she stopped and looked back. He was following close behind us. She knelt down and she waited for him to catch up.

He soon caught up.

"Willis, you can't come down to the beach with us. Now turn yourself around and walk back to the cabin. You have to stay back there with Mom and Dad."

He didn't say anything.

She got back up onto her feet. We walked down the path down through the trees, again. She looked back for him and he was still following close behind us. She knelt down there and she waited for him to catch up, again. He soon caught up to us. This time she took him by the shoulders and she shook him.

"Willis, I told you that you can't come down to the beach with us. So, turn yourself around and walk back to the cabin, like I told you."

"Jackie, please, can I go, too?

"No, Willis, you can't go, too. I don't want you with us."

"Jackie, I will be good. I promise you I will."

"No, Willis, you won't be good. You don't keep your promises to me. So, stop asking me to come and start walking back to the cabin."

He didn't move.

"Willis, I get so tired of repeating things to you."

She looked back at me, and then back at him.

"Willis, your stubbornness is driving me crazy! Well okay, fine; if it means that much to you, then come down to the beach with us. I'm sick of fighting with you about it. But, Willis, I'm warning you, if you act up, again, I'm taking you back to the cabin, myself."

"Jackie, I will be good. I promise you I will."

"Willis, don't say that, unless you really mean it."

"Jackie, I really mean it."

"Okay then, you can come down to the beach. But don't forget that you promised to be good. You said that you really meant it, too."

"Okay Jackie, Boo, Boo," he said.

He jumped up and down and clapped his hands. Jackie took my hand and started us walking down the path through the trees, again. She looked back for him and he was still following close behind us. She knelt there and she waited for him.

He soon caught up to her.

"Willis, I'm taking you back to the cabin. And, I'm telling dad how you're acting and I'm going to ask him to give you a good hard spanking."

Willis's face lost it color and his eyes got big. He wobbled on his legs and he fell backward down onto his butt and began to cry. Jackie took him into her arms and hugged him. She looked back at me and I shrugged and raised my eyebrows. Like her, I didn't know what was going on, either.

When Willis felt better she helped him get back up onto his feet. They held hands and they walked up to me. I held his other hand and the three of us walked down the path through the trees, together. We stopped on the bank above the lake and we stood and looked over it, lying flat and calm in the sunlight. Willis let go of our hands and he ran off down over it and down the slope of the beach to the boat. We followed him down over it and when we caught back up he was standing in it and looking it over.

"Willis, do you want me to take you for a boat ride?"

He looked up at Jackie.

"Jackie, can I go for a boat ride in Cortney's boat?"

"Yes, Willis, you can."

"Jackie, are you coming, too?"

"Yeah, I am. But first I'm going up and telling Mom, that we're going?"

"Yeah, okay."

She walked up the slope of the beach and she climbed up the bank and walked up the path through the trees. She came back down it and she climbed back down the bank and walked back down the slope of the beach to the boat.

"Willis, get back out of the boat, okay?" she said.

He got back out of it.

"Okay," she said, "let's all get a good hold of it and when Cortney says to push really hard on it, push as hard as you can. Okay, Willis?"

He both nodded, and smiled.

We all got a good hold of it.

"Okay, push as hard as you can," I said.

We pushed as hard as we could. Willis got himself all stretched out to where he was down onto his knees and almost lying down in the sand. We stopped, and we waited for him to get back up onto his feet.

"Okay, let's all give it one last big push," I said.

We all got another good hold of it and we gave it one last big push and Willis got himself all stretched out to where he was lying right down in the sand. We waited for him to get back up onto his feet and we all got another good hold of it and we all gave it another last great big push and watched as it slid down off the beach and out into the lake.

CHAPTER 7

WILLIS FIDGETED ABOUT AND WAITED TO GET IN.

"Here, Willis, let me help you in."

"Huh?"

I lifted him up under the arms.

"In you go," I said.

He squirmed about as my fingers slipped on his bony ribs.

"Sorry about that, Willis," I said.

I helped Jackie get into the boat and she sat down and she put her arm around his waist and as I was I pushing it off I stepped into the cold water and as I crawled in across the bow I felt it go down in under the arches of my feet and feel like ice on them. I half-crawled and I half-walked by them back to the outboard and I started it and I turned out toward the shipping lanes and as I throttled it up the boat climbed up out of the water and leveled off into a fast plane across the lake. Jackie's hair blew in the wind; her sunglasses propped up onto it I thought that she looked like a movie star. We sped out into the shipping lanes and we circled around a ship and ran back in toward the beach. Ahead of us now and up in under the trees was the cabin and back of it and a mile of still more trees the bluff, like a wall shutting off the village from the outside world. Jackie looked up at it. Willis looked behind us at the trail of our wake. I kept my eyes on the beach ahead and as we closed on it and when it got to where I either shut off the outboard or we crashed into it, I shut it off and swoosh, up went the boat up onto it stopping up high and dry in the sand.

Willis jumped out into the arms of his dad.

"Willis, be careful what you're doing."

He climbed him as though he was a tree.

"Willis, if you act like that, Cortney won't take you for another boat ride."

"Willis, I'm sorry for landing so fast?"

He ignored me.

"Willis, get down now and be a big boy."

Armand stood him down onto the beach.

Jackie pointed between us.

"Cortney, that's my dad, Armand. Dad, that's my friend, Cortney."

We both nodded, and smiled.

"Say, I watched you come in from out there," he said. "This boat of yours goes along pretty fast. But that outboard looks kind of small for it. But nowadays I guess they all look like that, eh?"

"Yeah, they do."

"But I hear they still have lots of horsepower?"

"Oh yeah, they do. That's a twelve horse Sea King. It's actually my Dad's boat."

"Oh, I see, uh-huh? He lets you use it whenever you want to, eh? Is that it?"

"Yeah, that's about it."

"Well, that's good of him. A guy can have a lot of fun out here with a boat. It looks like it's a good fishing outfit. Do you go fishing with it?"

"No, actually I don't. I mostly run around with it."

"Oh, uh-huh, I see? I did a lot of fishing when I was your age. I couldn't seem to do enough of it. I loved trolling for pike."

"Would you like to go for a boat ride?"

"Uh-uh," said Willis. He grabbed onto his Mom.

"Willis, let go of me and act your age."

She twisted herself free.

"Willis, Cortney, wasn't talking to you. He was talking to Dad."

He ran off up the beach.

"Cortney, maybe, later, eh? After my breakfast has had a chance to settle?"

"Sure, Armand, whenever you're ready to go," I said.

Bunny and Ellie walked up the slope of the beach. They climbed up the bank and they started up the path through the trees,

together. Shortly they came back down over it wearing their swimsuits, now. They both walked back down it to the boat. Neither of
them was tanned in the slightest. Both their arms and legs were a
ghostly pale white. Bunny asked me if we were going for a boat ride.

"Sure, whenever you're ready to go," I said.

We both smiled.

"Armand, Cortney's taking us for a boat ride. Come over here
and get into the boat with us, and go, too?"

He ignored her.

"Ha, ha. This is going to be fun. How fast does it go?"

"Oh, it goes along pretty fast."

She got into it.

"Mom, get back out. We have to push it into the water, first."

"Jackie, what did you say to me?"

"I said to get back out of it, so we can push it into the water."

"Oh, okay? That's what I thought you said."

She got back out of it.

We all got a good hold of it and we pushed it into the water.

"Jackie, I knew that we had to push it into the water, first; my
God, you always have to make me out to be so stupid? I was in it
looking it over, okay?"

Jackie said nothing.

"Ha, ha. Now we're ready to go. Armand, come over here,
and get into the boat with us, and go for a boat ride."

"Not now. Not until after my breakfast has had a chance
to settle."

"Oh, just get over here and get into the boat, and shut
that big mouth of yours. I'm sick and tired of hearing about your
weak stomach."

"I said that I would later. Not now. Now leave me alone."

"My God, everything is a big deal to you!"

Armand said nothing.

"You act like you're a hundred years old."

He ignored her.

She looked at Ellie.

"Ellie, get into the boat. You and I will go whether anybody else does, or not."

Ellie got into it.

She looked at Jackie.

"I already went," Jackie said.

She looked up the beach at Willis.

"Willis, get back down here and get into the boat, and go for a boat ride with your Momma."

Instead he ran back to his Dad.

"Okay, you stay here with your Dad, then," she said to him.

Jackie walked up to me.

"If you want to, we can go swimming when you get back?"

"Yeah, I do."

"I'll get into my swimsuit."

"Yeah, okay. If you want to, we can go out to the island and swim out there?"

"Yeah, I do. That sounds fun."

"Good. I'll hurry back."

"Okay. Don't be too long."

"No, I won't," I said.

We sped out toward the shipping lanes and I stood up to see where I could go out and sweep around the back of a ship and we went out to it and we swept around the back of it and I looked ahead to see where I could run up alongside it and go out front of it and sweep around the bow of it and we ran up alongside it and we swept around the bow of it, and ran back into the beach.

BOOK TWO

Showing Her Around

CHAPTER 8

BACK IN AT THE BEACH THEY GOT OUT AND SAID IT WAS A
nice ride and great fun and thank you very much, Cortney. I said I
was glad they liked it and it was my pleasure and Jackie got into the
boat and I dug an oar into the stones of the lake bottom and pushed
out to where I could start the outboard. I started it and I throttled
up and as we sped off up the lake shore, the island always in our
sight, we stayed far enough out to avoid the big rocks in along it
and the rocky shoal sticking out beyond Sweet's Point. We looked
out over the calm surface of the lake and we saw it as a bluish white
glare in the hot sun, our faces crinkling up into knots if we looked
at it too long or too hard. We looked in at the cabin that David
Sweet built for himself a hundred years ago, its rafters falling down
into it and leaning at angles against its inside walls, all its window
panes either broken or gone. We couldn't see any distance into the
dark openings between the cedar trunks to speak of, but we could
follow with our eyes the ridge of Nadoway Point out from the foot
of the bluff far out into the lake, its balsam glinting in the sun and
its birch standing out against the spruce of the bluff and then only
the occasional clearings of white sand and clumps of horse grass
and blueberry bushes, and the occasional thicket of hazelnut. We
cut out at an angle there to the island and we sped out straight
and fast to it and we idled into the prettiest bay of them all going
slowly into it and looking down through its fresh clear water at the
sandy bottom and off to either side at the broad sweep of its beach.
I always enjoyed taking a fresh look at it and at the beech and oak
trees stretching upward having large full tops. But what I always
liked to look at most were the old fish tugs pulled up with their
twisted and unshapely sterns hanging out over the water.

We landed among them.

I helped Jackie get out.

"It's really beautiful out here, eh?"

"Yeah, it sure is."

"It's like a graveyard for old fish tugs."

"Yeah, it sure looks like it."

"It makes me sad when I look at them."

"Oh, how's that?"

"They remind me of when fishing was good around here. I wish I was alive back then. It must have been really something to get up in the morning and go out and work on them all day, especially on a nice day like today?"

"Yeah, it probably was. But being that you're a guy, it's probably easier for you to imagine."

"Yeah, you're right. I guess it would be, eh?" One of the fish tugs was in better shape than the others. We walked over to it and we looked in through an open doorway at its rusty net lifter. "I'd like to fix this one up and take it up to the Naomokong, and live in it up there, and do some fishing with it."

"It looks big enough to?"

"Heck, yeah. It'd take a lot of work to get it back into shape. You'd have to go over everything. But if you put your mind to it and you stuck to it and didn't give up, you'd get it done. You'd have it, then. You could take it wherever you wanted to."

"Yeah, you could."

"You could take it out the St. Lawrence Seaway. All the way out to the Atlantic Ocean. That'd really be something, eh?"

"Yeah, it sure would."

"But out there you'd have to be careful. The storms are big out on the ocean. You wouldn't last very long out in a small tug like this. It looks big pulled up here on the beach. But out there it would feel small, especially out in a really big storm."

"Yeah, it would."

"It's funny how things work, eh?"

"Oh, how's that?"

"Well, we worry about getting caught out in a big storm. But we always manage somehow to get through them. Myself, I think it's the lulls in between them that are the problem. Before we can get over one, there's another one."

She didn't say anything.

"The world's a crazy place, eh?"

"Yeah, it sure is."

We both looked off at the lake.

The island has the shape of a figure eight. It's narrowest where the old fish tugs are pulled up. We walked up between them and we climbed up the bank and started to walk across it, going between the beech and oak trunks, crossing the clearings of white sand and their patches of blueberry bushes and clumps of horse grass, and the occasional thicket of hazelnut, and coming back out onto the inside and climbing back down the bank and walking down the slope of the beach to the water and sitting down in the warm sand above it and looking around ourselves at everything. There were waves of heat rising up out of the sand. The mountains across the lake from us looked like foothills. The trees rustled in the breeze behind us up on the bank. Other than for them there wasn't a sound. It was quiet enough to hear yourself think. Myself, I was thinking of my Great Uncle Dan, of his story about the Great Silence. He said that it was so loud that you couldn't block it out. That you could stick your fingers into your ears and you could still hear it. We didn't know whether to believe him, or not. After all who ever heard of a silence that was loud? It didn't make any sense to us. We looked at him like he was crazy and all he did back at us was grin. I was out hunting out in the woods alone when I heard it for the first time. It scared the hell out of me. I got back up and I got the hell back out of there. It reminded me of listening to a seashell for the first time. You needed to know what you were listening for to hear it. I haven't heard anything as loud, since.

"It's quieter out here on this side, eh?"

"Yeah, it is. It's deafening quiet."

I listened and I could hear the faint pounding of a big diesel off somewhere in the distance and, closer by, the wake of a ship running down the beach and curling down over onto it and washing up to the bank and after splashing up against it, the rinsing sound that it made as it ran back down through the sand and went back into the lake.

"I love it out here on this island. It's one of my most favorite places around here. I come out to it as often as I can."

"I can see why. It's like a paradise."

"Yeah, it is. It's a truly beautiful island, eh?"

"Yeah, it sure is," she said, and smiled.

We lied down in the sand on our stomachs. We put our heads down on our arms and we closed our eyes. She pushed herself back up with hers and she looked back out over herself at the lake. The sun's glare off it blinded her. She looked back down at the sand.

"That sun's glare off the water is blinding."

I pushed myself up and I looked back out over myself.

"Yeah, it sure is. It's hard to see anywhere?"

"Just the same, it's amazingly beautiful out here. Thanks for bringing me out to see it."

"You're welcome. I'm glad that you like it. I don't think that I could be a real friend to someone who didn't."

"It must mean a lot to you, then?"

"Yeah, it does. It's actually a big part of who I am, as a person?"

"Oh, really? You're lucky you live so close to it, then. This is my first time out here and I love it already. But you'd have to be crazy not to, it's that beautiful."

"Yeah, you would. Have you ever blissed-out?"

"Blissed-out?"

"Yeah?"

"No, I don't think I have?"

"I have, lying right here?"

"What do you mean, blissed-out? I haven't heard that, before?"

"You haven't, really? Well, it feels like there's a fireworks' going off in your head. It gets warm on the top of it and you get a little delirious."

"Oh, really?"

"Yeah, has anything like that ever happened to you?"

"No, I don't think it has."

"Well, if you go out into the woods and you sit still and don't move or think about anything else except for how beautiful it is there, it could happen to you. At least, that's when it happens to me."

"Oh, really?

"Yeah, really. Did what I said about being a real friend, sound funny to you?"

"No, actually it didn't. I knew what you meant. I've felt like that myself, before."

"You have, really?"

"Yeah, as I was writing a poem, I have."

"Then I'm not as crazy as I sometimes think I am?"

"No, I don't think you're crazy, at all?"

Neither of us said anything.

"How often do you come out here?"

"Well actually, this is my first time this summer. I used to come out four or five times a summer. I'd come out to where we are right now, and I'd lay down here all day, sometimes."

"You would, really?"

"Yeah, I would?"

"I've never been out to any island, before."

"You haven't, really?"

"Yeah, really? There aren't any islands in close to the Soo. None that you can get out to without a boat, anyway. And, I have never stayed out by a lake before where I could have."

"Where do you go swimming in there?"

"We go up to Sherman Park. But it's not as quiet as it is out here. There are always people around you, too. But it's the only place to go in there. The Soo doesn't have a swimming pool."

We sat back up. She looked down at her stomach for sand sticking to it. I looked out into the shipping lanes for the ship whose big diesel I heard earlier. She didn't see any sand and I didn't see the ship.

"Have you ever been swimming, up there?"

"No, I haven't. My dad took us up there to see the zoo when I was a kid. But we didn't go swimming."

I fell backward down onto the beach.

"That breeze up there has a cool edge to it. It's warmer down here in the sand."

I rolled onto my side and used my hand to prop up my head. The weight of it pushed my elbow deep down into the sand. She fell backward down onto the beach herself, now. She rolled onto her side and propped up her head, too. Her elbow also pushed deep down into it. She picked up a handful and she let it pour back out, making a small pile with it.

"Did it upset you? What I said to you about storms?"

She looked up at me.

"I thought that I was being clever, I guess, talking about your family, like that. I usually don't butt into other people's lives, that way. I actually don't even like people all that much, to begin with. I guess I was trying to tell you how I felt when I was down at the cabin with you. How with your Mom carrying on like she does, sometimes, and what with Willis doing all the crazy things, that he does? And, how you and Ellie fight all the time, like you do, sometimes, too, and what with the way that your Mom and Dad squabble like they do, a lot of times? Well anyhow, I guess I'm not all that comfortable when I'm down there with you?"

I wondered if I should have said it.

She took my hands into hers and she wrapped hers around them.

"Cortney, I knew what you meant. You don't have to explain anything to me."

"You did?"

"Yeah, I did. Cortney, my parents are who they are. They're not going to change for you or for me, or for anybody. And, there's nothing that any of us can do about it. But that doesn't mean that who they are has to have anything to do with us. We are who we are. We're not them. We have our own lives to live."

What she said made perfect sense to me.

"I get things mixed up, sometimes, eh?"

"Yeah, I think that you do. But that's okay, too."

I only heard her say, 'you do.' I was looking at her bikini. It fit her body perfectly.

"You look good in your bikini."

"Thank you."

"It fits you perfectly."

"Thank you."

"I haven't seen you wear it, before this."

She didn't say anything.

"Jackie, what's your nationality?"

"I'm French-American?"

"Oh, really?"

"Yeah, my parents came over here from France?"

"Then that's where you get your stonewhite skin, eh?"

"Yeah, it is?"

"Well, whatever your nationality, you're lovely all over."

"Thank you."

"Actually, you're exceedingly lovely all over."

"Thank you."

We both smiled a little.

I was on a roll. I sensed she knew it.

"I'm glad that we've met."

"I'm glad that we have, too."

We both blushed a little.

I waited for her to say something to me.

"My top's so big and my bottom's so small."

I didn't know what she meant, or what to say back to her. I let it go and I went on with my thoughts. "Did I sound serious when I said all those nice things to you? I really did mean them. I didn't just say them."

"I hope that you really meant them. It felt good hearing you say them to me. But then what girl wouldn't feel that way?"

We both blush a little, again.

I picked up a handful of the sand and I let it pour back out myself, now, making a small pile with it, too. I fell backward down onto the beach. I closed my eyes and I looked up through my eyelids at the sky. It was a fiery orange. I thought about my Dad. I wished that he didn't have to work away from home. I missed him so much that it hurt, sometimes. I blocked out the sun with my hands. I thought about my Mother. I wondered why she always worried so much about me. I could take care of myself. I wished that she would stop doing it. I imagined myself sitting in the college library and studying to be a lawyer. Someday, I would have my own law office. I looked over at Jackie. I loved her so much that it hurt, sometimes, too. I thought of the old fish tugs left behind to rot on the beach. About how they were symbols of broken dreams. About the hard-working fishermen who worked on them. I thought about the lamprey eel destroying the fish populations in the Great Lakes. I felt the sun on my belly and I wondered if Jackie could feel it on hers, too. I wondered how she could be both inside and outside of me. Of how the beach could be a big part of who I was as a person. Of how I could drink a few beers and I could glimpse my innermost feelings and learn what my true feelings were about everybody and everything in my life. Of how I could love nature so much that it hurt, sometimes, too. I wondered if she could understand that about me? Someday I will have to explain it to her, I thought.

"Cortney?"

"God?"

"Are you okay?"

"Huh, God?"

"Are you alright?"

I opened my eyes.

Jackie was leaning over me.

"Yeah, I'm alright. I'm okay?"

"Is there something wrong?"

"No, I'm okay."

"Are you sure?"

"Yeah, I'm sure. I must have been dreaming."

"Yeah, I think that you were. You scared me."

"Oh, I'm sorry."

"No, that's okay."

I sat up.

"Cortney, are you sure you're, alright?"

"Yeah, I'm alright." I looked out over the lake. The sun's glare off it blinded me. "Jackie, have you ever been lonely?" I said. "I don't mean a little bit lonely. I mean really terribly horribly lonely?"

CHAPTER 9

"NO," SHE SAID.

The way she said it it sounded so final that I felt cut off from talking to her about something important to me. I sat quietly beside her. I could only think of going.

"Are you ready to go?"

"Yeah, I am, if you are?"

"Yeah, I am. We've been out here quite a while. They're probably worried about us."

"Yeah, they probably are."

"We can come back out again later, if you want to."

"Yeah, I do. I love it out here."

We got back up and we walked back up to the bank, climbed it and walked back across the island, passing between the beech and oak tree trunks, crossing over the clearings of white sand and the blueberry bushes and the clumps of horse grass and, the occasional thicket of hazelnut, and coming back out onto the inside of it and climbing back down the bank and walking back down between the fish tugs.

"What kind of a nest is that?"

"It's a seagull's nest."

"It looks like it hasn't been used in a while."

"They all look like that this time of year."

"Oh, I wonder why?"

"They're still messy from last spring, when they had their babies in them."

"Oh, really?"

"Yeah, really."

"They're not together very long as a family, eh?"

"No, I guess not?"

"That's sad, if you really think about it. I hope they're all okay."

"Yeah, they most likely are," I said.

We walked the rest of the way down to the boat. We got into it and I took an oar and pushed out to where I could start the outboard. I started it and we idled out into the bay.

"Let's go slow?"

"Yeah, sure?"

"I get tired of going fast all the time."

She didn't say anything.

"If you go slow, you have time to look at things. You're not just speeding by them."

"Yeah, you do."

I looked back in at the island.

"It's a truly beautiful island, eh?"

She looked back in at it, too.

"Yeah, it is. I'm glad that you brought me out to see it. I've never been out to an island, before."

We both looked up at a seagull flying by overhead. We watched it fly in across the lake to the beach and fly back in over it and the swamp and up the face of the bluff and off into the pale sky beyond it.

"I still have another favorite place to show you. Would you like to see it?"

"Yeah, I would, very much so."

"Good. We'll go and see it, later, then."

I throttled up the outboard and I sped back in to Sweet's Point and as we came up on it I brought the boat hard-around, the starboard side rising, the portside sinking and, sliding sideways across it now, we bounced back over our wake and we lost all our speed and stalled dead in the water. Her smiling back at me, me smiling back up at her, the propeller spinning freely, the motor racing wilding, I throttled the outboard back down and as the propeller caught again I throttled back up and as we climbed back up out of

it we sped off back down along the lake shore and out front of the
fishery again, we turned back into it.

CHAPTER 10

WILLIS RAN UP TO THE BOAT.

"Jackie, did you have fun?"

"Yes, Willis, I did."

"Where did you get the flower?"

"Willis, I got it out on the island, where'd you think I got it?"

"Can I hold it?"

"No, you can't hold it. But if you don't touch it, you can look at it." She held it out to him and he touched it. She pulled it back. "Willis, I said not to touch it."

"What kind of a flower is it?"

"Ellie, it's a carnation? Can't you tell?"

"How did they come to grow over there?" Armand said.

"My Aunt must have planted them over there," I said. "Her husband was a fisherman. He built a cabin back in behind where all the old fish tugs are pulled up on the beach."

"Humm, that's interesting?"

"Yeah, it is. Their cabin's gone, now. But the flowers are still growing back in there."

Bunny asked to see it and Jackie handed it to her. She smelled it and she handed it back.

"Jackie, take it up to the cabin," she said, "and put it into a glass of water."

"Right now, Mom?"

"Yes? Can't you see that it's wilting, already?"

"Yeah, I can? But Courtney and I want to do something, first."

"Jackie. I'll walk up with you. Okay?"

"Can I go, too," Willis said. "Can I carry the flower?"

"Yes, Willis, you can. But first you have to promise me that you won't touch it? If you touch it, it will die."

"Jackie, I promise you I won't," he said.

She handed the flower to him. He held it with both hands and walked up the path through the trees. Halfway up to the cabin he touched it.

"Willis, if you touch it, it will die. Please don't touch it, again! Okay?"

"Okay, Jackie, I won't?"

"If you don't touch it, you can still carry it. Okay?"

"Yeah, okay," he said.

Inside the cabin she took the flower from him and she put it into a little glass of water and she sat it up on top of the refrigerator where you could still see it and it was safe.

We stepped back and we looked up at it.

"The flower is pretty in its own little glass of water sitting up on top of the refrigerator where you can still see it and it's safe, isn't it?" she said.

"Yeah, the flower is pretty in its own little glass of water sitting up on top of the refrigerator where you can still see it and it's safe, isn't it?" Ellie said.

As both Jackie and I looked at her her face turned red.

Willis held up his hands to Jackie.

"Jackie, lift me up. So I can see it, too?"

"Willis, you carried it up here? You saw it, already."

"But I want to see it, again."

Jackie ignored him.

"If it's okay, I'll do it?"

She both nodded, and smiled at me.

I lifted him up and I held him by it.

He looked at it and I put him back down.

He held up his hands to me, now.

"Cortney, please? Please, again, okay?"

"Willis, you saw it, already," Jackie said.

"But I want to see it, again," he said.

I lifted him up and I held him by it, again. He looked at it and I put him back down; but this time onto my shoulders. I carried him outside, that way.

He held onto my head.

"Oh no, oh no," he said.

"Willis, I got a good hold of you, you're okay," I said.

I walked down the path through the trees with him. I stood him down on the bank and he ran down over it and where it leveled off with the beach fell face first down into the sand.

He got his mouth full of it. He lay there spitting it back out.

"Willis, get back up and run out into the lake, and wash out your mouth," Jackie said.

"He shouldn't have opened his mouth," Bunny said.

Willis got back up and he ran out into the lake.

"Bunny," Armand said, "why did you have to say that to him? My God, you're his mother. He got his mouth full of sand?"

"Oh, shut yours," she said to him.

"Armand, we can go for that boat ride now, if you want to?"

"Yeah, let's do that."

"Don't forget about us going swimming?" Jackie said.

"No, I won't."

"Don't be too long, okay?"

"Yeah, okay. We'll go out to shipping lanes and we'll come right back in."

"Cortney, I'll push us off, okay?"

"Yeah, okay, Armand. Thanks."

I got into the boat.

"Daddy, can I go, too?"

"Yes, Willis, you can. Get over here, and I'll put you in."

Willis walked over to his dad and he lifted him up. But before he could put him into it he began to cry.

"Willis, why are you crying? You asked Dad to go?"

"Not now, okay? I don't want to go, now. Okay?"

"Willis," Bunny said, "stop that crying and be a big boy."

Armand stood him back down onto the beach.

"You stay here with your Mother, then," he said to him.

Armand pushed the boat off the beach. He climbed in over the bow and I started the outboard. I turned out toward the shipping lanes and as we sped out into them I looked back in at the beach. Willis was standing back on it and watching us go, and crying. I checked our course ahead and I looked back in again and he was still standing back on it, and watching us go. But I couldn't tell anymore if he was still crying. We were too far out now; what a pity, I thought, that no one knows what to do for him. Jackie is right: he needs to be taken to see a doctor. I held our course out into the shipping lanes ahead and we went out into them and circled around the back of a ship and we ran up alongside it and we went out in front of it and turned back in to the beach. We sped back in toward it and as we came up on it I throttled the outboard back and as the stern settled down into the water the bow rose up and our wash rushed in from behind and lifted us and shoved us up onto the beach where we bumped to a stop.

Armand stood up to get out.

"Say, Cortney, that was quite some ride. I liked that view from out there, too" he said. "You'd have to see it yourself, to believe it could be that big."

"Yeah, you would."

"Thanks for taking me out to see it."

"Armand, you're very welcome," I said.

He got out of the boat and he walked over to the big log. He stood by it and he looked off into the woods.

"Say, what's the name of that big hill that you can see back in behind us, here?" he said.

"Oh, that's the Mission Hill?" I said.

"Oh, uh-huh? That's what I thought it was, the Mission Hill."

He sat down onto the big log, now. He looked back out into the shipping lanes. He's probably thinking back over our ride out into them, I thought. Now Jackie walked up and she said something to me about us going swimming.

CHAPTER 11

"CORTNEY, ARE YOU GOING SWIMMING WITH JACKIE?"

"Yes, Willis, I am."

"I already went swimming."

"Willis, don't bother Cortney."

He walked off up the beach.

Jackie and I held hands and we walked out across the sharp slippery stones near shore. We eased our feet down onto them and we swung our arms every which way and we leaned forward and back and this way and that and kept our balance, and didn't fall. We got out to where the water was up to our waists. The bottom was sandy and it felt good under our feet.

Farther out Ellie was down swimming in it.

"Ellie, is the water cold out there?"

"No, it's not cold. But it's not warm, either."

"BURR, it's really cold in here."

I splashed myself with it.

"Cortney, what are you doing?"

"I'm splashing myself with the cold water. It helps you get used to it."

She stood up.

"It doesn't feel as cold when you're down in it."

"Then why did you stand up?"

She made a face at me and I made one back.

"Let's all jump down into it, together. Okay?"

"I was down in it, already."

"I wasn't," Jackie said.

"Let's all do it, together, okay?" I said.

"I like taking my time and getting used to it, first," Jackie said.

"Oh, Jackie, come on," Ellie said. "Just do it, too? Okay?"

"No, it's too cold to."

"It doesn't feel cold when you're down in it."

"Then get back down in it?"

"You'll get used to it faster, that way."

Jackie shook her head, no.

"I like taking my time," she said.

I frowned without meaning to.

"Okay, maybe I will," she said, "to get it over with."

"I'll count up to three," I said. "At three, we'll jump down into it. Okay?"

They both nodded, and smiled.

"Well, here goes?" I said. I counted to three. At three we jumped down into it. Wow, it was cold. It felt like ice on me. But I stayed down in it and I didn't get right back up. But when I looked at them they both were back up and on their feet already. They were hugging themselves and shivering as the cold water ran back down off them and went back into the lake.

"If you get right back up, you'll never get used to it," I said.

They both sank back down into it.

"I'm used to it, already," I said.

They both made a face at me.

A stone splashed into the water near us. We looked back in at where it splashed and back in at the beach. Willis was back, and he was picking up another stone. He stood back up and he threw it out at us, too.

It too splashed into the water by us.

"Mom, Willis is over here throwing stones at us. Will you please call him over there with you?"

Bunny hollered for him and he ran back up the beach.

"I think he just wants attention."

"If he does it again, let's ignore him. Okay?"

. "Why doesn't he come swimming?"

"He's afraid of the water. He only goes out to his knees."

"Oh, that's too bad?"

"Yeah, it is. He could be having fun."

Jackie splashed Ellie with the cold water and she dived down into it. When she came back up Ellie splashed her back. We splashed each other and we screamed and hollered as the cold water hit us. We swam out to where it was over our heads. Out there we would have to get used to it. We dived down to the bottom and we looked for flat stones to bring up and skip across the lake. We found some and we brought them up and as we were skipping them across it another stone splashed into the water near us. We looked back in at where it splashed and back in at the beach, again. Willis was back and he was picking up another stone to throw. He stood back up and he threw it out at us, too. When it too splashed into the water back in where we were swimming we ignored it and we dived back down to the bottom and looked for still other flat stones to bring up and skip across the lake.

CHAPTER 12

IN THE WINTER I GO OUT ONTO THE LAKE WITH MY DAD
and I help him set his nets under the ice. We lift them in the mornings and we pick out the fish. We don't wear our gloves. He thinks
that it tears the mesh in them. First my hands get cold and then they
get numb and finally ice gets on them. I cuddle way down under the
blankets of my bed at night and I dream of swimming with a pretty
girl. It always helps me to feel warm against my cold bedroom.

I thought it was funny how dreams come true.

"A penny for your thoughts," she said.

"Huh?"

"A penny for your thoughts?" she said, again.

It took a moment for me to understand what she said. It took
another one to decide if I wanted to tell her.

"Well, I help my Dad set his nets on the lake in the winter.
When we lift them in the mornings we don't wear gloves. He thinks
that it tears the mesh in them. My hands get so cold that ice forms
on them. I cuddle down under my blankets on my bad at night and
I dream of swimming with a pretty girl, and lying on the beach with
her. It helps me feel warm in my bedroom."

"You did, really?"

"Yeah, I did? You look like the girl in the dream. The first
time that we went swimming, together, I felt like we already went
swimming, together."

"You mean like in De' a Vu?"

"Yeah, like in that."

"That's funny. Because that's happened to me, before, too."

"Has it really? Was there ever anybody in them like me?"

"Well, not exactly like you. But like you, just the same. But
then I only had the one dream, too."

"Well, when it happens to you, you swear to God that it happened to you, before. You get big goose bumps all over you."

"If you want me to, I'll tell you about mine?"

"Yeah, I do. I would really like to hear it."

"Well, okay? But it wasn't anything like yours?"

"That's okay? I'd still like to hear it."

"Well, it happened to me last winter. I got a candle making kit from my mom for Christmas. I was making candles with it and I got this strange feeling. Like I made those exact very same candles, before."

"You did, really?"

"Yeah, I did?"

"What was that word you used for it, De' a Vu?"

"Yeah, De' a Vu?"

When I scratched my arm she asked me if I was itchy.

"No, I'm not, why?"

"What you're doing right now then, it wasn't in your dream?"

"You mean us talking about it, like this?

"Yeah."

"Actually it wasn't, why?"

I saw you scratching your arm and I thought maybe it was."

I didn't say anything.

She giggled a little.

"Tell me, when you get big goose bumps all over you, again. Okay?"

"Oh, I don't know? I'll have to think about that?" I said.

We both giggled a little, now.

I dived down into the water. I stayed down near the bottom. I swam in the opposite direction of what she saw me dive. She was standing with her back to me when I came back up. I stayed down in it and I waited for her to look around for me. She looked around herself and she saw me.

"My God, Cortney," she said, "you swim like a fish. I was beginning to think that something terrible happened to you. That you got caught under the water on something."

I dived back down into it and when I came back up I was back in front of her.

"Do you have big goose bumps all over you, now?"

"I'll never tell?" I said and smiled.

"Oh, you do, don't you?" she said. "I can tell by your smile?"

"Well, I might, but then I might not, too. But either way, I'm not telling you."

She giggled a little, again.

"Jackie, what are you giggling so hard about?"

"Nothing, Ellie?"

"Well, Your Highness, please excuse me for asking?"

"You're excused."

"Cortney, I'm going to ask you again later. Okay?"

"Yeah, okay. But I'm not going to tell you again later, either."

She made a face at me and I made one back.

She was the pretty girl in my dreams. I did have big goose bumps all over me. But I wasn't about to tell her that. Not after seeing how she could see through people. Earlier I was showing her all the ways that I could swim. But now I didn't feel like swimming, anymore.

"You ready to go in?"

"Yeah, if you are, I am?"

"Yeah, I am."

"Ellie, we're going in, now."

"Yeah okay, I am too, then."

We waded back in to the beach, together. We came out at the big log where both Bunny and Armand were sitting.

"Don't go anywhere, girls. We'll be leaving soon."

"We won't, Mom."

We walked up the slope of the beach. We climbed up the bank and we walked up the path through the trees, together.

"Dad promised Mom that he's take her up to the Tahquamenon Falls," she said. "It's going to be an early birthday present for her. Her actual birthday isn't until next week."

"Oh, uh-huh?"

"Yeah, she wants to eat up there, too."

"When will you get back?"

"It probably won't be until after dark."

We both stopped walking. It was the first thing that she said to me about it. I didn't know what to say back to her.

"If you want to, you can come up to the cabin with me while I get ready. We won't be leaving for a while, yet."

"I should probably go home?"

"You're not going to come up with me?"

"No, I guess not."

She didn't say anything.

"I'll come back down in the morning. Okay?"

"Yeah, okay?"

I didn't say anything.

"I'm sorry," she said, "that I didn't mention it to you."

"That's okay. I'll come back down in the morning, and, if you want to, we'll go for a walk, somewhere."

We can walk up into Sweet's Bay, I thought. We can look for agates up there. Until then I will find something else to do. I will walk over and see Bill and tell him about the girls, again. It wouldn't be a good idea to go up with her. I wouldn't be comfortable waiting for her to leave. It was better to go home and to get it over with.

"I'll come back down in the morning and, if you want to, we'll go for a walk up into Sweet's Bay."

"I'm sorry that I didn't mention it to you," she said, again.

"If you want to, we can look for agates up there."

"Yeah, okay."

"I'll talk to you later, then, okay?"

"Yeah, okay. See you," she said.

She walked up the path to the cabin and I cut off it into the woods.

CHAPTER 13

I WALKED OUT THE DRIVEWAY AND I CUT OFF IT ONTO A birch and balsam ridge. I walked up it to where I figured I was above the big log. I walked back down through the trees to the beach and as I walked out onto it I looked down it at the big log. It was empty, now. Bunny and Armand were up at the cabin getting themselves ready to go, now, too. I looked out into the shipping lanes. There weren't any ships in it. They're probably bunched up somewhere riding out a big storm in the lee of an island, or a point of land, I thought. I imagined them all having sunk. All the sailors on them having drowned. I cringed at the thought of them still being in it. I walked up along the lake and I turned up the slope of the beach walking through the deepening sand with my shoes sinking down into it and I went up pass where my dad keeps his boat pulled up onto the long skids and I climbed up the bank and walked out the beach road and stopped at the blacktop. I crossed it and I jumped the ditch and I walked through the yard and up to the outhouse, and in. I sat down on the seat and I leaned back on the wall and looked out over the swamp. The dark clouds above it looked like mountains. I wondered if Jackie could see them from up at the falls. If I owned an airplane I would fly over her and find out, I thought. At the edge of the swamp a sparrow was hopping through the branches of a tamarack tree. It was catching insects and eating them as it went. I love watching them swooping through the air in perfect formation. I love watching a tamarack tree swaying in the breeze together with a spruce and a birch tree in the sunlight after a fresh December snowfall, too. In my mind there's nothing prettier in all the northland. As I got up to walk across to the house the sparrow startled and flew off into the swamp.

I went inside.

My Mom looked up at me and set her book aside. "Well, look whose back home, already. My, what a pleasant surprise, this is?

What may I ask brings you back so soon? I didn't expect that I would see you for at least another day?"

I sat down on the couch.

"You look a little down in the face, today? Is there something that's wrong? Is it something that I can help you with?"

"No, I'm okay."

"Maybe, it's none of my business?"

"Is there anything to eat?"

She was always asking me questions.

"I was getting up to make something for us as you came in the door. Are you still going to be here?"

"Yeah, I am."

"Good. I'll make enough for the three of us, then."

She made supper for us and she put it on the table. We sat down and we ate it and got back up. They stayed behind in the kitchen and I walked out into the living room. I sat down on the couch and I watched the evening news. They washed the dishes and they came in and sat down with me and watched it, too. After it they both got back up and they went off upstairs, together. I watched a sitcom and I got back up and went off upstairs, too. I got undressed and I got into bed and went off to sleep. But all through the night I kept waking back up. In the morning I got up still tired. I got dressed and I went down into the kitchen and ate breakfast with my Mom. I went out the door as she began to pick up the dishes. I walked out through the yard and I jumped the ditch and got out onto the blacktop. I crossed it and I walked down the beach road and pushed my boat into the water. I got into it and I took an oar and shoved it out to where I could start the outboard. I started it and I sped off down along the lake shore. Out front of the fishery I brought it hard-around and I sped back in and landed on the beach. I jumped out and I ran up to the bank and I climbed it and ran up the path through the trees to the cabin. Jackie and Ellie were outside standing in a clump of birch trees.

CHAPTER 14

ELLIE SAID HELLO.

"Hi, Ellie."

We both smiled.

"Hi, Jackie."

"Hi."

We both smiled, now, too.

"What are you guys up to?"

"Actually, we're not up to anything?"

"What are you talking about?"

"Actually, we're not talking about anything, either."

They both raised their eyebrows.

"We've been standing here waiting for you."

"Do you realize what I did? I asked you guys three questions. Now you can ask me three, if you want to."

They both raised their eyebrows, again.

"You did what?"

"I asked you three questions?"

They both said 'oh?', and smiled.

Now, we all of us smiled.

"More truthfully," Jackie said, "we haven't been standing here waiting for you. Actually, we've been standing here waiting for you and wondering what was taking you so long, too. We thought that you would be here sooner."

"Saturday is my mother's grocery shopping day. I went into town with her. How was your trip up to the falls?"

"It was okay," Ellie said.

"It was just okay?"

"Yeah, I'm not impressed by waterfalls, I guess?"

"Jackie, what did you think of them?"

"I thought they were beautiful."

Ellie strode off to the cabin.

"I'm going inside where it's warm," she said. "It's too cold out here for me."

Jackie eyes flashed. "I think she's jealous?"

"I still have another favorite place to show you. Would you like to see it?"

"Yeah, I would, very much so?"

"Good. Do you like climbing up big hills?"

"Yeah, I guess so."

"Good. You'll like climbing up this one, then. It's really big. It goes straight up four hundred feet."

She smiled at me.

"Okay. But first, I have to go in and tell my mom?"

"Yeah, okay."

She went inside of the cabin.

She came back out wearing a sweater.

"In case it gets cold," she said, and smiled. She got into the boat and it tipped and reaching out she grabbed onto the sides managing to sit down on the middle seat and I got into it myself and it tipped under me too and I made my way by her back to the outboard and reaching out to the sides managing to sit down too I took an oar and pushed us out to where I could start the outboard and I started it and sped off down along the lake shore.

CHAPTER 15

I HELPED JACKIE GET INTO THE BOAT. I PUSHED IT OFF AND I climbed in over the bow. I half-walked and I half-crawled by her back to the outboard. I started it and I throttled up and sped off down along the lake shore. Out front of where the old logging road went back in off the blacktop to the bluff I came hard-around. I sped back in to the beach and we got out and walked up it to the bank. We climbed it and we walked up the path through the trees to the blacktop. We crossed it and we walked back in on the old logging road to the foot of the bluff. We stood there and we looked up at it. It narrowed down into a trial as it went up across the face of it.

"It looks steep, eh?"

She didn't say anything.

"It is, too. You got your climbing shoes on?"

"Hardly," she said, and smiled.

We held hands and we started up it. We climbed up to a tree down across it and we climbed over it and sat down and took a break. We could see out over the treetops, already. The lake was like a huge bowl of summer blue water sitting out in the bright sunlight. It went out and away in every direction. We turned our heads to see all of it.

"It's truly a big lake, eh?"

"Yeah, it is."

I looked up at the trail.

"We've got a long climb ahead of us."

She looked up at it, too.

"Yeah, we do," she said, and smiled.

We held hands and we started up it. We climbed up to another tree down across it and we climbed over it and we sat down and took another break.

"The people that owned the sawmill built this road. They used it to haul their logs down to it."

She looked up at it, again.

"You go up fast when you're actually climbing, eh?"

"Yeah, you do."

We held hands and we started up it, again. We got up to where the bluff leveled off and you walked back in to where the trail went back up it. We sat down there and we looked out over the lake.

"I like the way that the breeze scurries across the water and just touches it here and there," she said.

"Yeah, I do, too."

I pointed out into the shipping lanes.

"See that ship, out there? It looks like it is going slow, eh? But see how the water is curling up off the bow? It's actually going about thirty miles an hour."

She looked out at it and off over the lake, again. She pointed out to Parisian Island.

"There's a lighthouse on that island?"

"Yeah, that's the Parisian Island Lighthouse. It's on the Canadian side of the lake."

She looked out at it.

"You ready to hit it, again?"

"Hit it?"

"Yeah?"

"Yeah sure," she said, and smiled.

We held hands and we started up it, again.

"Years ago a ski club came out here from the Soo. They used this old logging road to climb back up to the top. They cut all the trees down off the face of the bluff."

She looked down at it.

"Looking down at it now, you wouldn't know it, would you?"

"No, you wouldn't. The trees grew back fast."

We climbed up to the next tree down across the trail and climbed over it. But instead of stopping above it and taking another break we kept going. Shortly we were at the top.

"How are your legs feeling?"

"They're feeling, okay?"

"Mine are tightening up. I climb the bluff every year but in between times I forget how steep it is. Before I remember to slow down and take it easy, they're tightening up, again."

I looked down at the beach for the boat. I wanted to show her how far we come since leaving it. But I couldn't see it. It was down below the lake's tree line. I looked out across Whitefish Bay. The breeze was still scurrying across the water and just touching it here and there. The Parisian Island lighthouse was still a white dot on its shoreline. Now a ship was slowly making its way up the shipping lanes.

"My Dad sailed on the lakes."

"Oh, he did? How did he like it?"

"He actually hated it."

She didn't say anything.

I looked back down at the trail.

"We've come up a long way?"

"Yeah, we have."

"I'm glad that we're up at the top. I don't think that I could go much farther."

"No, I don't think I could, either."

We sat down in the shade of a tree. We looked out over the treetops. They were like a lush green carpet on the land. They went out to the summer blue lake. This, I thought, is why we live up in the northland. This lush green forest and the summer blue lake. When we go for a ride out into the country the road is ours. When we walk out into the woods it is ours, too. We stretch our muscles and we breathe in the fresh air and feel as good as we possibly can. But we each knew what it meant to live up here, too. That your chances of finding a good-paying job were slim to none. That when you found one you held onto it for dear life. That you would rather lose an arm or leg than it. I looked down at the old fish tugs pulled up onto the island. I helped my Dad and Wayne pull up theirs onto it for the last time. Fishing was giving out on the lakes, by then. The lamprey eels were reducing the fish populations to almost nothing. It was next to impossible to make a decent living at it, anymore. I looked down at the old sawmill back in by the bluff. I remembered working at it. Like the old fish tugs, it was going to hell, too. The family that owned it moving away. I looked down at the fishery. Its buildings were also going to hell. You worked at the Indian casinos, nowadays. Those in the Soo or in the Bay Mills Indian Community. Or out at the state prisons in Kincheloe where the wages were a little bit better. You learned to live with life's bare necessities. You built your own house, heated it with your own wood, put in your own sewer and planted your own garden, and hunted and fished and picked berries and canned and did whatever else it took to stretch out your paycheck through the week. Sooner or later you came to hate the northland as much as you loved it.

CHAPTER 16

JACKIE POINTED OUT ACROSS THE LAKE.

"Those mountains look close enough to reach out and touch?"

"Yeah, they do."

"Why is it like that? Do you know?"

"No, I don't know. But it could be that the air is clean over the lake."

"Yeah, it could be. At least it sounds like it could be."

She pointed down the lake.

"What's that way down there?"

"Oh, that's the International Bridge. You can only see the top of it."

"Really?"

"Yeah, really?"

"Then that over there must be Soo, Ontario?"

She pointed to it.

"Yeah, it is. And, that over there," I pointed to it, "is Soo, Michigan. And, if you look back of us," I pointed back of us, "you can see the island."

She looked back of us.

"Wow, it looks different from up here, eh? It's not the perfect figure eight that I thought it was. It's not as big as I thought it was, either."

"Yeah, someday the middle will wash away. Then there will be two islands?"

She didn't say anything.

I began to unlace my shoe.

"I'm going to dump out the sand."

She began to unlace hers, too.

"I'm dumping out mine, too."

"How are your legs feeling, now?"

"They're a little sore, now?"

"Mine are sore, now, too," I said.

We dumped out the sand. It was white on the green grass. We lay down under the tree and we looked up through the branches. The sky above us was a beautiful summer blue. It went out and away and off into forever.

Something crossed my mind.

"I come up here and I sit down and look down at the roofs of the houses, down at the wall of green trees on the face of the bluff, out across the lake at the mountains in Canada and, as I'm doing it, my whole life passes before my eyes; the places where I've been, what I did when I was there, and who I did them with. It happens to me every time that I come up here."

She didn't say anything.

"This is the only place that it ever happens to me. I promise myself to come back up sooner the next time but then I forget to, and I don't come back up again for another year. I like it up here as much as I do out on the island, especially on nice days, like today."

"It's truly beautiful up here, eh?" she said.

"Yeah, it is. I wanted my dad to build a house up here when I was a kid. But as I got older I gave up on the idea. I guess I realized how cold it would be to live up here, especially during the winters."

She didn't say anything.

"Sometimes when I think about our winters I feel that we'd all be happier living down south somewhere."

"Yeah, I do, too."

I didn't say anything.

"I like how you think about things like that. It's one of the things that I like most about you?"

I didn't say anything.

"What keeps you from coming back up here?"

"I'm not really sure."

"What do you think about when you look out over the lake?"

"I think about a lot of things. But it's kind of a long story, or I'd tell you about it."

"Well, tell me about it, anyway. I'd really like to hear it."

"Are you sure?"

"Yeah, I am, very much so."

"Well, if really want to hear it, I'll tell you about it, then. It starts when my sister and me were still kids and my Dad arranged this airplane ride for us. We squeezed into the back seat of his friend's small Piper Cub. We flew down along the bluff here (I pointed out at about where we flew by) to the lighthouse where he tied his plane down for the night. I remember looking down at the roofs of the houses and at the paths going between them and imagining myself running back and forth on them. I looked down at where we played kick-the-can out on the beach road and where we sat around the campfires in the woods and smoked the cigarettes that we stole from our folks and, as I was looking down at everything, I felt like I was looking down at a picture on the floor. I was never up in an airplane before and when I saw how small our village looked it really bothered me. Back down on the ground I tried not to think about it, again. But I couldn't stop myself. It got to the point to where if I was playing kick-the-can out on the beach road and I looked back at the bluff, I'd think about it, again. It still bothers me when I look back at it."

When I looked back at her she was staring at me. I stopped telling the story to her. Considering the short time that we knew each other I decided that it was enough for now.

"Well, I guess, that's enough of that?" I said.

She didn't say anything.

"It's funny how one thing can change the way you look at your whole life, eh?"

She didn't say anything.

"We should probably get started back, eh?"

"Yeah, my Mom's probably worrying about us?"

I pulled up a handful of the grass. I rolled it back and forth between my hands. I smelled it and I made a wish with it and threw it out over the bluff.

"It took us so long to get up here, I hate to go back down."

"Yeah, I do, too. But knowing my Mom, I think we better. She might call the sheriff, and report us missing, or something?"

We both chuckled a little.

"I've never known anyone like you?"

"Oh, how's that?"

"The way that you feel so strongly about things?"

"Oh, what's wrong with that?"

"Well, there's nothing wrong with it? It just scares me the way that everything is so important to you."

I didn't say anything. But I wondered what scared her about it. She looked at me to see how I was taking her. I looked back at her regretting that she said it. It was part of who we were as a couple, now. If we stayed together we would have to live with it.

"Remember what I said to you out on the island about feeling lonely. And, how I didn't say anything back to you about it. Well, I thought about it since then and I decided that it was because you didn't like people."

"Yeah, I remember us talking about that. But I didn't say that I didn't like people. I said that I didn't like them all that much?"

"Oh yeah, you're right. I forgot. You did say that, didn't you?"

As we walked back down the trail I thought back over what we said. It was our most serious disagreement to date. Our feelings were bruised in it. I looked out across the lake at the mountains in Canada. They did look close enough to reach out and touch. She was right about that, I thought. But she wasn't right about everything being important to me.

Everything wasn't important to me.

CHAPTER 17

WE WALKED SLOWLY BACK DOWN THE TRAIL. WE DIDN'T
want to go too fast and to trip and fall down over the trees down
across it. We took a step and we went to put our foot back down
onto it and when it wasn't there our foot went further down it and
it plopped back down onto it and shook our whole bodies. It took a
lot less time to go back down it than it did earlier to go up.

Jackie's side hurt her at the bottom.

"It feels like needles sticking into me."

"Put your hand on it, and push in."

She did it.

"Is that helping it, any?"

"Yeah, it is a little?"

I walked off the side of the road and I sat down on a stump.

"Come over here and sit down by me. That'll help it, too."

She walked over, and she sat down by me.

We both looked off into the trees.

"Is that helping it, any?"

"It's hard to tell. But I think it is, a little."

"Good. Mine's almost gone, now. Let's rest here before we
start out." I raised my arms above my head. "Raise your arms up,
like this."

She raised them up.

"Is that helping it, any?"

"Yeah, it is a little."

"Good, keep them up like that. Maybe it will go away."

She kept them up.

We both looked off into the trees, again.

"Is it feeling any better, yet?"

"Yeah, it is a lot. I can barely feel it, now."

"Good. Let's rest here for a while, yet."

"Where'd you learn how to fix side-aches?"

"I learned it by myself. I kept trying different things until I found what worked."

"Well, you're good at it. Thanks for helping me with mine."

"You're very welcome," I said.

We walked out the old logging road. Where the cedar met overhead it felt like we were walking through a tunnel. The sun was blocked out. There were dark shadows everywhere. We got out to the blacktop and we crossed it and started down the path through the trees. We stopped on the bank and we looked out over the lake, lying below us flat and calm in the sunlight. I reached out for her and when she came into my arms we kissed and hugged and looked deeply into each other's eyes. I felt closer to her, in that briefest of moments, than I ever felt to anyone else before or since. We climbed down the bank and we walked down the slope of the beach, together. We pushed the boat into the water and we got into it and I took an oar and pushed out to where I could start the outboard. I started it and I throttled up and we sped back up along the lake shore. Out front of the fishery I brought it hard-around and we sped back in to the beach. They all were down on it in their swimsuits, now. All, except for Armand, that is; he was still dressed in his street clothes sitting off by himself on the big log. When I tried imagining him wearing a swimsuit and I couldn't, I wondered if he even owned one.

Bunny walked up to the boat.

"Hi, Cortney."

"Hi, Bunny."

We both smiled.

Armand waved over to me.

I waved back. "Hi, Armand," I said.

I looked at Ellie. "Hi, Ellie."

"Hi, Cortney."

We both smiled, now, too.

"Girls, don't go anywhere. We'll be eating soon."

"We won't, Mom."

"Jackie, are we still going swimming, or what?"

"Yeah, Ellie, if you still want to, we are?"

"Well, I've been waiting here all morning for you to get back, so that we could?"

"Well, let's get ready and go, then."

"Well, you didn't mention it to me? I had to ask you about it."

"Well, if you still want to go, we'll go?"

"Well, ever since you got back you've been acting like you still don't want to. And, if that's the case, then I still don't want to, either. If you knew that you were going to be so long, you should have said something to me about it. I wouldn't have sat here all morning waiting for you to get back, so that we could. Well okay, if you still don't want to go swimming, then we won't go."

I butted in...

"It doesn't sound to me like either of you really know what you still want to do. And, if that's the case, then I think that you both need to think about it some more. And, if after you do, and you still can't decide whether you still want to go swimming, or not, then I think that you should still go. After all, Ellie did sit here all morning waiting for us to get back, so that you could."

"Cortney, what are you saying?"

"Oh, nothing. I'm trying to be helpful. After all, I was the one who wanted to go swimming in first place. And, being that I was, I'm inclined to agree with Ellie. I think that we should still go swimming."

"Well, okay. But now she's acting like a brat about it. And, now that she is, I'm not so sure that I want to go anywhere with her."

"Jackie, I asked you if you still wanted to go swimming, that's all?"

"Yeah, but you were rude to me about it. And, now that you've been rude to me, I don't still want to go anywhere with you."

"I wasn't rude to you about it."

"I'm sorry, Ellie. But, yes, you were."

Ellie shrugged, and walked off.

"Okay, fine then," she said, "I'm not going to talk to you about it, anymore. If you still don't want to go swimming, we won't go."

Bunny walked up the slope of the beach.

"Girls, I'm going up to start lunch, now."

"Mom, do you want us to come up and help you?"

"Yes, Jackie, that would be nice of you."

"Did I hear that right, Jackie? Did you ask your Mom if we could go up and help her? Did you ask her to be nice? Or did you really mean it?"

Bunny stopped walking. She looked back at Ellie.

"Ellie, you'll be eating with us, too? Why shouldn't you come up, and help?"

"Well, I wasn't invited out here to work? I was invited out here to go on vacation?"

"Well, Ellie, we're all out here on vacation. Not just you. That is, if you want to be technical about it."

Ellie didn't say anything.

Bunny climbed the bank. She started up the path through the trees.

"Ellie, if you get her mad at us, again, we'll never go anywhere by ourselves, ever again."

"Jackie, I'm not getting her mad at us, again. Besides, who gave you the permission to talk for both of us. Thank you, but I can talk for myself. Go up and help her if you want to. Just leave me out of it, okay?"

They both looked off at the lake.

CHAPTER 18

JACKIE DROPPED TO HER KNEES.

"Let's build a sand castle, together?"

She began to push the dry sand aside.

Ellie and I walked up to her and we dropped to ours, too. We helped her push it aside. Willis walked up to us and he dropped to his, now, and began to help. We all worked hard, and cleared off a big place to build the sand castle. We built its walls, first, making them both thick and tall. We didn't want anybody to climb over them, or to knock them down.

Willis sat back on his legs and looked between us.

"My hole's empty."

"Willis," Ellie said, "your hole's not empty, is it? Your hole still has sand in it, doesn't it?"

He didn't say anything.

"Willis," said Jackie, "stop being funny, and get back to work!"

I sensed that he was holding back about something.

"Willis," said Ellie, "get some sand out of your hole and put it on the wall!"

Willis put his hand back down into his hole. He brought up a handful of sand with it. He patted it onto the castle wall and began to smooth it out.

"Girls, I can use your help, now."

Bunny was above us on the bank.

"Okay, Mom. We'll be right up."

"I wonder," Ellie said, "if she really needs it, or if she just wants it," Ellie said. "It's probably bothering her that we're not up there helping her?"

They both got up onto their feet.

"If we don't go up," Jackie said, "she'll get mad at us, again. And, you know what that means? That we'll never go anywhere by ourselves, ever again."

They climbed up the bank, together.

"Cortney, we'll holler at you when it's time for you to come up. Okay?"

"Yeah okay, Jackie. Thank you."

They walked up the path through the trees, together.

"Willis, are you having fun?"

He didn't say anything.

"Do you like building sand castles?"

He ignored me.

"No one will climb over these walls, or knock them down, eh?"

He said nothing.

The hell with him, I thought. He could at least try and be my friend. After all I was his sister's boyfriend. I decided to ignore him, too. If he won't talk to me, I thought, I won't talk to him, either. I didn't say another word to him, or even look at him, again.

"It's time to come up and eat, now."

Jackie was above us on the bank.

"Yeah, okay, Jackie," I said.

"Willis," I said, "let's go up, and eat, now."

He ignored me, again.

"Willis, come up and eat, now," Jackie said.

He ignored her, again, too.

"Dad, Willis won't get up and come up and eat with us?"

Armand got up onto his feet.

"Will you please bring him up with you?"

He walked over to him without saying anything. He was bending down and picking up Willis as I climbed the bank. I held Jackie's hand and the two of us walked up the path through the trees, together. Halfway up to the cabin we heard them coming up over it. Willis was crying his lungs out.

"My God, that kid has gotten to be a spoiled brat!" Jackie said.

I didn't say anything.

As we went inside Bunny looked up at us.

"We're having BLTs for lunch, today."

We walked over to the table and we sat down at it. Bunny picked up the platter of bacon and lettuce and tomatoes, and passed it to Ellie.

"Ellie, take what you want. There's lots of everything."

Ellie took what she wanted, and she passed to us. We took what we wanted, and we passed it back to Bunny. She set it back down on the table in front of her. She picked up the platter of butter and mayo and cucumbers and passed it to Ellie, too. Armand came in the door carrying Willis now. He wasn't crying, anymore. But when he saw his Mom he started back up.

"Willis, will you please stop that crying," she said to him.

Instead, he cried louder.

Armand carried him over to the table and he sat him down at it. He sat down beside him, and he took a slice of toast off the platter and put it onto Willis's plate. Bunny took a slice of tomato off it and she put it onto his toast. Armand added three slices of bacon to it. Bunny added two leaves of lettuce. Armand put a slice of toast on the top of it and he cut it in two. Willis picked it up and as he began to eat it both Armand and Bunny began to make BLTs for themselves. We all of us were soon busy eating. When Ellie wanted another one Bunny passed the platters around the table, again. Jackie and Ellie talked about their trip up to the falls. Jackie was still excited about seeing them. But Ellie wasn't. She didn't think that they were anything special. She thought that the rustic restaurant where they celebrated Bunny's birthday with a big birthday dinner was special. She loved the big stone fireplace in it. Willis asked his Mom how old she was, and when she smiled at him and she said that she was thirty-nine, the rest of us looked around the table at each other and smiled. Jackie asked her what it was like to get old and when she told her that forty-nine wasn't considered old anymore we looked around it at each other and smiled, again. Now Ellie asked her where she was born and when Bunny told her in a small Northern Ontario town and she went on about what it was like to grow up there Armand cut in on her and he asked her what the weather was going to be like for the rest of their vacation. When she told him that it was going to be both sunny and warm the rest of us looked around at each other and smiled and both shouted and clapped our hands.

Bunny looked down the table at me. She saw that my plate was empty.

"Cortney, do you like apple pie?

"Yeah, I do, Bunny. Thank you."

"Jackie, get up and go out into the kitchen, and get a piece of apple pie for Cortney."

Jackie pushed her chair back and she got up from the table. She left for the kitchen and as she went into it the others at it looked up from their plates at me. She came back out of it carrying my apple pie and they looked back down at them. She brought it over to me and she put it down in front of me and sat back down herself. I picked up my fork and as began to eat it I could feel all their eyes coming back on me.

BOOK THREE

She Goes Back Home

CHAPTER 19

THE WATER WAS WARM IN ALONG THE BEACH IN THE sandy shoals and we watched the sun go down below the line between the lake and the sky and it light up like it was on fire and as the darkness came in slowly around us we stayed down in it and we kept warm, and there was nothing else. Bunny called from up on the bank that it was time for the girls to come in now and she turned around and walked back up the path through the trees to the cabin. We waded in and we walked back in across the sharp slippery stones near shore and we went up the slope of the beach and climbed up the bank and walked up the path through the trees to the cabin ourselves, now. Outside the door Jackie and I kissed out in the cold dark and as she went inside I started off for home, the thought of bears always on my mind and my eyes always on the lookout for them and, when I didn't see any bears but only the dark shadows that I thought could be bears, I raised my hands up to my lucky stars above and thanked whatever Gods there be. I walked along through the black night cold and shakily with only my t-shirt on for warmth my shoes and trousers in my hands and, too dark to see the opening of the road through the cedar ahead, I held my arms out in front of me in case I bumped into a bear. I hurried up to the house and I went inside and hurried up the stairs to bed and went off to sleep. In the morning I got up and I got dressed and went downstairs into the kitchen and I sat down with my Mom and we ate breakfast, together. As she picked up the dishes I walked out the door and hurried out through the yard and got out onto the black-top and walked down it and, when I got down to the cabin I went swimming in the fresh clear water of Lake Superior with the girls and lay down on the beach in the sunlight and took little snoozes with them and, when we any of us got bored or we felt too alone, we nonsensed each other and we horsed around and went on long careful walks up and down the beach looking for agates, and artful pieces of driftwood. We lived through our days very well like that and we used them up very well and when they were over with we none of us had any regrets. The feeling was always with us to use them up well because we all of us knew that summer would soon be over, and that fall would soon be upon us. And, as unbelievable as after a long hard cold winter when you're outside in your t-shirt for the first time on the first truly warm day of spring and it feels like seventy but it's only thirty, it was Saturday, now.

Sunday, they were going back home.

Saturday was my mother's grocery shopping day. I rode in to town with her and Aunt Margaret. They dropped me off out front of Hall's Jewelry and went on themselves over to the IGA Supermarket. As I went in through its heavy glass door I looked to either side at the display of rings and watches. I didn't see any that I liked and besides, they all cost too much, anyway. The old white-haired woman standing inside greeted me and as I returned it to her the heavy glass door slammed shut behind me. I described Jackie to her and what I wanted to buy her.

"Humm?" she said.

She didn't scratch her chin, but she put her hand up to it. She leaned forward as if to listen to me with one ear more than the other.

"Humm?" she said, again.

I sensed that she was ready to say something else.

"Well, let's see? What is it that we can we find for the dear young girl that you describe to me?" She walked down the row of showcases to where she looked like she had something in mind. She stopped at it and she looked down into it and she bent down and brought up a necklace and showed it to me. But it wasn't quite what I wanted. She showed me another one, but it wasn't quite right, either. She went up and down the showcases doing that, first those on this side of the long narrow room, then those on that. "Humm?" she said. "Surely we must have something in here that's right for her?"

She pursed her lips and she put her finger on them and she pointed with another finger in at the items that she thought Jackie would like to have, and looked up at me.

"No," I said, shaking my head.

She pointed in at something else.

"No," I said, shaking it, again.

"No," I said, after she pointed in at still something else.

She took items out from another showcase and she handed them up to me one at a time and as I set them down on top of it she straightened up from her crouched position straining as she rose from it as if it took her every ounce of strength that she had while at the same time rubbing her back with a hand on either side of it.

"Do you have any idea at all what it is that she likes in jewelry?"

"No, I'm sorry, but I don't," I said.

"Oh?" she said, pursing her lips.

"No, I'm sorry," I said. "But we've never talked about it."

She seemed to be completely lost, now. She looked back down into the showcase. "Would she like a bracelet, like this, instead?" She brought up a bracelet from it to show it to me. She put it into a black plastic box and she set it on the top of it.

I looked in at it picking it up with both hands to do it.

"No, I'm sorry, but I don't think so," I said, setting it back down.

"Oh?" she said. She set out seven other bracelets, each one a little different than the one before it. "Maybe she will like one of these, instead?" she said, doing her best to smile.

I frowned slightly. "No?" I said.

She brought up a box with a broach in it.

"Or, maybe, she'd like a broach rather than a necklace?"

She looked in to my eyes as if to plead with me. I felt as if she was begging for me to like it. Then, she talked to herself more than to me. "Now, what would the sweet young girl that you describe to me, like?"

She got up and she walked to the next showcase. I followed along behind her. She looked across it at me.

"Do you see anything in here?"

I looked in at the items.

"No, I'm sorry. But I don't see anything."

"You say that she's a smallish girl?"

"Yes, she's barely five feet tall."

"Humm?"

"Yeah, she's actually both small and tiny."

"Oh, okay?"

She was looking in at the rings, now. She brought out five rings and she set them down on the top of the showcase.

"How about a ring like one of these?" she said. "Do you think that there's one among these that she would love to have?"

I looked them over carefully.

"No, I'm sorry, but I don't think so. One of them maybe, but no, I don't think so."

I was beginning to feel bad for taking so long. She on the other hand seemed to be getting her second wind. She must have realized that it wasn't going to be a quick sale and adjusted herself to it. Myself, I wanted the gift to be perfect. I didn't know what it would be, but I thought that I would know it when I saw it.

She moved on to the next showcase and I followed along behind her.

"We have some lovely necklaces in here," she said. "Maybe there's a necklace in here that she'll love." She bent down, and she came back up with four necklaces. I leaned over the showcase and I looked in each box. She moved on to the next showcase. "I'll tell you what I'm going to do," she said. "I'm going to go along here and set out pieces that I think she will like, and you can come along behind me and look at them. Maybe that way we will find something?"

I straightened up to listen to her and to acknowledge her directions.

"Sure, that should work fine."

She began to set out things onto the next showcase.

"I'm sorry for being such a problem," I said. "I guess I should have asked Jackie, and got an idea of what she liked."

"Oh, that's okay," she said. "You wanted it to be a surprise, and it might have tipped your hand."

"Well actually you're right," I said. "I was worried about both those things. I want to surprise her with a going away present. Her family's been vacationing out where I live and she's going back home in a couple days, and I do want it to be a surprise."

She looked at me, but she didn't say anything. She walked across the back of the room and she began up the other side of it. I finished looking at the pieces on one showcase and I moved on to the next. Then, I crisscrossed the room going back and forth between the showcases and looking in at a ring or a broach or a necklace which caught my eye. It was a long and time-consuming process, but I eventually narrowed down to two necklaces and a ring. A short while later I narrowed down further to the two necklaces. In the end, I choose the delicate gold necklace with a white pearl cupped in a golden oak leaf. I took it over to her in its black plastic box.

I handed it to her.

"I'll get this necklace."

Eagerly taking it from me her face suddenly gladdened.

"Well, let's see what you're buying for the dear sweet thing," she said, looking in to the box. "Well, it's beautiful. It's perfectly beautiful. I'm sure she's just going to love it."

She walked into the small office off the back of the showroom, where she began to wrap it. I followed along behind her.

"You don't need to wrap it."

"You sure? It's no trouble to?"

"No, it's alright unwrapped," I said.

"Okay then. That will be forty-five dollars and eighty-four cents."

I took the right amount from my wallet and I gave it to her. She took it from me with a big smile of gratitude.

"Thank you for your business," she said, "I'm sure that she's just going to love it."

"Thank you," I said, and picked up the box.

I put it into my trouser pocket on my way back out the door. All I could think of now was walking over to the grocery store and showing it to my Mom and if they were done with their grocery shopping riding back home with them and walking down the black-top and seeing Jackie. I was so caught up in my thoughts about her that I didn't hear the heavy glass door slam shut behind me as I did on my way in earlier.

CHAPTER 20

AT HOME I HELPED MY MOM CARRY THE GROCERIES INTO
the house. As she was putting them away I went back out the door.
I walked out through the yard to the blacktop and I walked down
it. It rained while we were in town. The rainbow colors were back
in the tarry spots. I got down to the cabin and Willis was outside
playing in the clump of birch trees, He was pushing his cars around
in them.

I walked up to him without being noticed.

"Hi, Willis. Is Jackie here?"

"Huh?"

He looked up for me.

"Is Jackie here?"

He jumped up to his feet and he ran for the door.

"Jackie, Jackie, Cortney's out here."

"Okay, Willis, I see him," she said, starting out.

I smiled at her.

"Here I am," she said, smiling back. She raised her arms and
she let them fall.

"It's good to see you, again,"

"It's good to see you, again, too."

We both smiled a little.

Willis ran back to his cars. He dropped to his knees and skidded in the dirt and came to a stop at them.

"What's new, if anything?"

"Actually, nothing is new."

As she said it her tooth moved a little. I ignored it and I went
on with my thoughts. "I'm sorry I'm late. Did you miss me?"

"Yeah, I did. Where were you?"

"I was in town with my Mom. It was her grocery shopping
day. Would you like to go for a walk?"

"Sure, where to?"

"Wherever you'd like to?"

She didn't say anything.

"I'm a great one for walking, eh?" I said.

"Yeah, you are," she said. "But I am, too."

"Yeah, you're a great walker, too?" I said.

We both smiled a little, again.

We walked out the driveway, together.

"What have you been up to?"

"Actually, I haven't been up to, anything?"

"Not anything, at all?"

"Well, not absolutely, not anything. I've been helping my Mom with packing. We're getting things ready for when we leave tomorrow."

"Hum, its' gotten close, now, eh?"

"Yeah, it has. Actually, too close."

I didn't say anything.

We stopped out at the blacktop and we looked both ways.

"Which way should we go?"

"Either way is okay by me?"

"I have another favorite place to show you? Would you like to see it?"

"You still have another one?"

"Yeah, I do. It's back in on an old logging road."

"Good, let's go and see it, then."

We started walking up the blacktop.

"See that old road up ahead of us?"

I pointed up to it.

"Yeah, uh-huh?"

"It goes back to an old saw mill. Or maybe I should say what's left of an old sawmill? There's actually very little left of it."

"I'm anxious to see it?"

"Good. I worked at it when I was a kid. Well, I didn't actually work at it. My friend worked at it and I helped him. He gave me some of his pay. His dad owned the place."

"Oh, uh-huh?"

"Yeah, it's just a short walk back in to it."

She looked up ahead of us, again.

"I always wondered what that old road went to," she said.

The old logging road was made of sawdust hauled out from the mill. You walked back in on it and your shoes sank down into it and it spilled down in over the sides of them. It went down in under the arches of your feet and it was so bothersome that you stopped and emptied it back out. We started to walk in on it. The sawdust spilled down in over the sides of our shoes. It went down under our arches of our feet. It was so bothersome that we stopped, and emptied it back out. The road went on ahead up through the cedars and swung to the left. We put our shoes back on and we walked up where it swung. We looked ahead of us, and we saw where it swung back to the right. We started to walk up there. Where the cedar met overhead the sun was blocked out. There were dark shadows every-where. It was cool. It felt like we were walking through a tunnel. We got up to where it swung back to the right. We stopped and we looked in to the clearing ahead. The old saw mill was in the center of it. I brought out the black plastic box.

I held it out to her.

"I got this for you."

"What is it?"

"It's a going away present that I got you."

"Oh?"

She took it from me and she opened it.

"I got you a necklace."

She took it out of its box. She handed it to me and I put it around her neck.

"Do you like it?"

She didn't say anything.

She held it up to her face. She looked at it and she took it back off. She handed it back to me. She bent her fingernail back and she let it go, making a snapping sound with it.

I wondered what could be wrong.

"Do you like it?" I said, again.

She didn't say anything.

I thought I heard her sniffle. I looked at her eyes and there were tears in them.

"Jackie, why are you crying?"

She didn't say anything.

She took out a tissue and she wiped her eyes.

"Jackie, are you okay?"

"Yeah, I'm okay," she said.

"Is it something I did?" I said.

"No," she said.

"What's wrong, then?" I said.

"It's nothing, really," she said, "I'll be okay in a second."

"Are you sure?" I said.

"Yeah, I'm sure," she said. "I'll be alright."

I figured that she would be. So I didn't say anything else. I was back in to the old mill a thousand times, before. There wasn't anything that I didn't know about it. There wasn't much left of it to show her, anyway. The old road went into the clearing ahead. It passed by the old mill and it went back in to the bluff where it circled and came back through. I looked in at the rail carriage that carried the huge heavy logs through the big circular saw. It was falling down in on itself. The circular saw was both rusted and pitted. I looked in at the old tool shed where I ran when the rail carriage broke down and got the tools to fix it. It too was falling down in on itself. The only thing left of it was a big pile of old broken lumber. The horse barn was still standing. But it was leaning far over to one side. The whole place was a wreck.

"Well, that's the old saw mill, for you."

She didn't say anything.

"Or at least what's left of it?"

She still didn't say anything.

I figured he wasn't quite herself, yet. But I wasn't quite myself yet, either. I imagined handing the black plastic box to her. Standing there and watching her take out the necklace. She handed it to me and I put it around her neck. Her face lighted up. We held hands and we stood there and looked in at the old sawmill. I told her everything that I knew about it. How my friend worked at it. How I helped him a little. How he gave me some of his pay. That his Dad owned the place. I told her about the men that traded their labor for lumber to build their houses. I wanted to tell her about the old woman at the jewelry store, too. About how hard she worked to find the right gift for her. About how happy she was when she found the necklace. But now I didn't feel like telling her any of it. Instead, I took her hand and I tugged on it and started us walking back out of there.

CHAPTER 21

WE WERE BACK AT THE CABIN WHEN IT STARTED TO COME out.

"Well, you are going to come and see me, aren't you?"

"Yeah, sure I am."

"Well, you have never said anything to me about it?"

"Well, I took it for granted that you'd figure I would."

"Oh?"

"Yeah, I did?"

"Well, I've wondered and wondered about it. You never said anything to me, and I didn't know what you were going to do."

"Is that what's been bothering you? Why you're so upset?"

"Well, we never have talked about us, after tomorrow?"

"Oh?"

"Well, Cortney, we haven't. I don't want to sound critical, but we haven't."

She had made a good point, because we hadn't.

"After all, I am going home in the morning."

"Yeah, you are, aren't you?"

"Yes, I am..."

"Well, it's only thirty miles to town. If you want me to, I'll come in and see you every day."

"Well, that's part of what I want to hear."

"Oh? What's the other part?"

"Well, actually, other parts, I think."

"Okay, the other parts, then?"

"Well, not any one thing in particular. But things in general. Like how we're going to see each other later. Other things, like our plans for being together?"

"Oh, okay?"

She took her hand back out of mine and she held it out to me.
I put the necklace back into it. She held it up to her face and she
looked at it, again.

"Cortney, I absolutely love it."

"Good, I'm glad that you do."

"It's so delicate and so tiny and fragile."

"Like somebody I know."

She blushed and looked off.

"Do I get a kiss?"

She looked back at me and tipped up her face. I pulled her
in tight to me and I kissed her once long and then six little times.

"Hmm, thank you."

We both shivered from the cold, now. We walked across the
driveway over to the fishery. We stood in the entryway and we
pulled up our collars, and snuggled up close.

"I wish I owned a car."

"Yeah, I wish you did, too."

"It would solve a lot of problems for us?"

"Yeah, it would."

"I kick myself now when I think back about Detroit. I should
have saved up some money."

"Yeah, uh-huh?"

"I told you about that, eh?"

"Yeah, you did."

"But I needed the clothes? Mine were worn out?"

"Yeah, they were. Besides, you didn't know me then, or that
you'd need a car."

"Yeah, you're right. We'll just have to figure out how to get
one, eh?"

She didn't say anything.

I goggled-eyed her.

"Cortney, don't do that." She slapped my shoulder. "We're
talking about serious things? You can be so silly, sometimes?"

"I'm sorry," I said, and smiled.

"Okay, I forgive you. But anyhow, have you made plans to get a car?"

"Yeah, actually I have. I should have told you."

"Well, darn you? You made plans to get a car, and you didn't tell me?"

"No, I guess not. I'm sorry again, okay?"

"Darn you, Cortney? You never tell me anything?"

"Oh, Jackie, I do, too?"

"No, Cortney, I'm sorry, but you don't. Now tell me about them before you forget to, again."

"Well, maybe now I won't."

"Darn you, you're teasing me, again?"

"Do you really want me to?"

"Yes, I do. So please stop teasing me, and tell me."

"Well, okay. But promise me something, first?"

"Oh, what's that...?"

"...that you will listen attentively."

She slapped my shoulder, again.

"Darn you. Now please hurry, and tell me."

"Okay, I'll talk. I mean, I'll tell?"

"Cortney, sometimes you can be so aggravating."

"Okay, I'm sorry, again. I'll tell you, now. Okay?"

"Yes, okay, please do?"

"I found myself a job. Now I can save up some money to buy a car."

"Wow, you really did? You actually found a job?"

"Yeah, I did."

Wow, that's so wonderful."

"Yeah, it is, eh?"

"Where's it at? What will you do there?"

"It's up at the resort. I'll be waiting tables, up there. I start this Thursday, already."

"Wow, Cortney, that is such great news."

"Yeah, it is, isn't it? It's close to home, too."

"Wow, what a wonderful surprise. It couldn't have happened at a better time for us, too."

"Yeah, that's for sure."

"I didn't even know that you were out looking for a job. It's all so great, eh?"

"Yeah, it sure is?"

"What will your schedule be?"

"I'll be waiting tables weekends, six to ten. Weekdays, I'll be doing maintenance work, twelve to five."

"Oh good. We can still see each other."

"Yeah, we can. Things are really starting to work out for us, eh?"

"Yeah, they sure are. It's all so great?"

"Yeah, it sure is."

We kissed and hugged, again.

"Until you buy it, you can still hitchhike into town and see me."

"Yeah, I can..."

"Well, good, you have been making plans for us? I feel so good about everything, now. Things are working out."

"It sure looks like it?"

We kissed and hugged, still again.

I noticed her arm was trembling.

"Your arm is trembling?

She felt hers and then mine.

"Yours is trembling, too."

"I should probably go home, and let you go in?"

"No, I'm alright?"

"But I'm keeping you out here?"

"No, I'm alright. I'll be okay."

"But we're both freezing to death?"

"Okay, you can go. But promise me something, first?"

"Oh, what's that?"

"That you will dress yourself warmer. Am I going to have to dress you, too?"

I didn't say anything.

She took my arm and she shook it.

"I know you through and through, already, don't I?"

We both blushed a little.

I watched a dust devil start out in the driveway. I mentioned it to her and we both watched it as it grew strong and began up it, picking up leaves and scattering them about as it went. It crossed the blacktop and it broke up as it went off into the woods.

"What makes them spin, like that? Do you know?"

"No, I don't know."

"I don't, either."

"Today's our last day of vacation, out here."

"Yeah, I was thinking about that, earlier?"

"Mom's getting up early. She's in a hurry to get back home. Dad starts back to work, tomorrow. If he wasn't, we could stay out here for another day, and maybe even longer."

I didn't say anything.

"He could drive back and forth to work, if he wanted to."

"Yeah, he could. But I doubt that he wants to, eh?"

"No, he doesn't?"

We watched another dust devil start out in the driveway. It grew strong and it started up the driveway, too, picking up leaves and scattering them about as it went. It crossed the blacktop and it also broke up as it went off into the woods.

"School starts soon."

"Yeah, it does."

"I still have school clothes to buy."

"Are you anxious to start back?"

"No, actually, I'm not."

"I don't blame you. I wouldn't be, either."

"Are you still thinking about college?"

"Yeah, I am. But not as much as I was."

"Well, maybe after the summer's over, you will again?"

"Yeah, maybe. There's still lots of time, too. It doesn't start until October?"

"Do you really want to go?"

"Yeah, I do."

"Well, maybe you will, then? At least that's how it works for me. I usually end up doing what I really want to."

"Well, I really want to go, so maybe I will then?"

"Yeah, if that's the case, you probably will?"

"But I still don't have enough money to."

"Well, maybe you will by then? There's still lots of time."

"Yeah, you're right. But whatever the case, I'm not going to worry about it. If I have the money to go, I will. If I don't have it, I won't. It's as simple as that. I'm going to live my life one day at a time, and take what comes."

"Yeah, I think that's best?"

"Yeah, I do, too."

I kissed the top of her head. She looked up at me and I kissed her lips. As I kissed them both long and hard I felt myself go off somewhere and come back. I told her about it and I asked her if that ever happened to her, too, and she said that it did. We walked back across the driveway and we stood outside the cabin door and kissed and hugged. I felt myself go off somewhere and come back, again.

We said goodnight.

"Sweetheart, I love you."

"I love you, too, Cortney."

"I'll come down early tomorrow. Okay?"

"Yeah, okay. We won't leave until you do."

She went inside, and I started off for home. As I walked down the path through the trees to the beach I thought back about my high school graduation. We walked across the stage and the principal handed our diplomas to us and congratulated us. We walked to the back of the gym and we lined up across the back of it. We waited there for our families and friends to come back and congratulate us. The girl standing next to me began to cry. I asked her why she was crying, and she said that it was because she was so happy. I took a step back and I made my way over to the exit door and went out it. I never liked school and I never felt that it liked me, either. I struck off down the road for home. As I walked I sensed something brewing inside me. I didn't know what it was. Back at home lying on the couch watching tv I felt it even stronger. In the morning I got up and I pulled on my clothes and walked out to the blacktop. I stuck out my thumb and the first car to come along stopped for me and picked me up. I was on my way down to Detroit. My cousin Ken had invited me to come down and stay with him when school got out. I had vowed to myself do it. I had forgotten about it since. But I was on my way now and now that I was I was determined to leave my old life behind and to find myself a new one.

CHAPTER 22

DOWN ON THE BEACH THE BREEZE OF THE ENTRYWAY was a strong wind. The waves washed up the slope to the bank. There was no place left above them to walk and keep your shoes dry. I walk down through them when that happens to me. I walk along the water. I still get my shoes wet down there but the sand is hard and it's easy to walk. Two thousand-footers were up bound in the shipping lanes, tonight. They use them to haul crushed coal down to the big city power plants. I looked out at them and I wondered what the sailors were doing. I imagined them sitting around the big folk 'Sal table playing a game of cards. What a hell of a way to earn a living, I thought. I turned up the slope of the beach and I walked up to the bank and climbed it. I walked up the beach road looking at the big picture window glowing in the dark ahead. My mom was still up watching tv. I crossed the blacktop and I jumped the ditch and went through the yard and up to the door and in. My Mom looked up at me. I walked through the living room and I didn't look back at her and I climbed up the stairs to my bedroom. I got in to bed but I lay awake thinking about Jackie for the longest time. I closed my eyes and when I opened them back up the sun was shining through my bedroom window. I got up and I got dressed and went downstairs into the kitchen. I sat down at the table with my Mom and we ate breakfast, together. As she picked up the dishes I went out the door and walked out through the yard. I got out onto the blacktop and I walked down it. When I got down to the cabin they were sitting out in the car waiting for me.

I walked up them.

"Hi, Jackie."

"You got here just in time."

"I'm sorry I'm late."

"That's okay. I'm glad you made it."

"I better say good bye?"

"Yeah, okay."

"I'll call you later, okay?"

"Yeah, okay. Please do. I'll wait for you to."

"Okay, I will. I promise you to."

The car began to move.

She reached out, and touched me.

"Good-bye, Cortney. Call me later, okay?"

"Yeah, okay, I will. Good-bye, Jackie."

"Good-bye, Cortney."

"Good-bye, Jackie."

"Bye," the others said.

They waved to me and I waved back.

"Good Bye," I said, to them.

Jackie waved to me, again.

I waved back to her as the car went out the driveway. It stopped out at the blacktop and it turned in toward the Soo. It disappeared in behind the spruce trees. They were on their way back home. After all the time that we spent together and after all the things that we did and after coming to know each other and to feel as if we would always be together they got into their car and they drove out to the blacktop and they stopped at it and turned in toward the Soo. They were on their way back home. I looked over at the cabin and I thought about sitting at the table and eating lunch with them. I looked over at the birch trees and I thought about standing out in them and talking to her for what felt like forever. And, as I did it the sad truth about summer sank in, it was over, now. We wouldn't eat in the cabin or stand out in the birch trees or walk down the path through the trees to the beach or cuddle up out of the wind in the entryway of the fishery, ever again. I thought about the way that things happened to you: they didn't happen to you and you waited for them to happen to you and when you were about ready to give up on them ever happening to you, they suddenly happened to you. They seemed to have happened fast when you thought back about them and they left you to wonder it they had happened or if you had imagined them. I thought about standing outside the cabin door and kissing and hugging Jackie and feeling myself go off somewhere and come back. I got down to the beach and I stood on the bank and looked out over the lake, lying flat and calm in the sunlight below me. I imagined the sun's glare off it as a blanket over it. I imagined the clouds above it as a ceiling to it. I thought about my Grandpa Bill warning to us not to hang on to things. That the world would go on without us. That we would get left behind. That if we ever caught back up to it we could find ourselves almost anywhere. Me, I was setting with my back up against the bank above where my dad kept his boat pulled up onto the long skids. I was looking out across the lake at the mountains in Canada. When I heard the kids playing in the water out front of me, I startled. When I heard somebody moving up on the bank behind me, I startled, again.

"Are you sleeping?"

"No, I'm not? Why?"

"Are you here, alone?"

'No', I wanted to say, 'Can't you see? I am sitting here with my Mom and Dad.'"

"Yeah, I'm here alone, why?"

"I just wanted to know."

It was my old girlfriend, Delores.

"Why are you asking me?"

"I thought that you were sleeping? I've been waiting here for you to wake up."

"Oh, you have been, eh?"

"Yeah, I have."

I figured she just got there. I knew Delores all my life. She lived down the road a couple houses from me. The truth was never good enough for her. She always lied to you a little bit whether she needed to, or not.

"I didn't want to startle you."

"Well, you did, whether you wanted to, or not."

"Oh, I did. I'm sorry. I didn't mean to?"

"I've been sitting here thinking about someone," I said, lying to her, to get even with her for lying to me. She didn't say anything back to me. So, I turned and I looked up at her.

"Her?" she said.

Why, I thought, did I have to say that to her? Haven't the two of us hurt each other enough?

"Actually, I don't remember who I was thinking about," I said, lying to her, again. Then, not satisfied with that, "Actually, I wasn't thinking about anyone. I've just been sitting here relaxing."

"You don't have say that you weren't. I know that you were."

I said nothing.

"But we're not together, anymore. So, it doesn't matter, now."

I said nothing, again.

"I'm going swimming up the beach. Do you want to come with me?"

"Me?"

"Yeah, uh-huh?"

"No, I really don't think so, Delores. But thanks for asking me, okay?"

"I don't want to go up there, alone."

"Dolores, are you for real? Do you really think that's a good idea?"

"Well, we're just going swimming, aren't we?"

I didn't say anything.

She came down the bank and she stood by me. Her bikini bottoms almost touched my face.

I pushed her leg a little.

"Please don't do that."

"Don't stand so close to me, then."

She took a step away.

"I'm sorry," I said, not meaning it.

She frowned as she walked down to the water's edge. She stopped, and she picked up a handful of stones. She looked through them and she tossed them aside. Her legs were long for a girl her height. They were creamy white where they came out of her bikini.

She bent over, and she picked up another handful of stones. As she did her butt pointed at me. It was hard to look at it and not think of all the evenings that we spent alone, together. She looked through them and she tossed them aside, too. She turned toward me and as she bent over and picked up still another handful of stones I saw her boobs hanging free in her bikini top. The nipples were erected on them.

"Go somewhere else, and look for agates."

"Why? What's wrong?"

"Just go somewhere else, okay? Your being here bothers me."

"Oh? I'm sorry. I didn't know?"

"I was here first, okay?"

The hurt look came back over her face. She straightened up and she walked off up the beach. She stopped up there and she bent over, again. Her hair fell down over her face. The sun was blocked out. She looked sad in the dark shadow of it. Suddenly, I didn't want to be there, anymore. I got up and I climbed the bank and I walked up the beach road wondering why I had to go and hurt the people that I loved. I crossed the blacktop and I jumped the ditch and I went through the yard and up to the outhouse, and in. I sat down on the hole and I leaned back on the wall and looked out over the swamp. The bluff behind it was like a wall shutting off the outside world. When I felt better I got back up and went across to the house.

Inside, my Mom looked up at me.

"Well, look who's back home? What may I ask brings you back so soon? I didn't expect to see you for at least another day?"

I didn't say anything.

She raised her eyebrows.

"What does this mean? Something good, I hope?"

I ignored her.

"Has something happened to upset you? Is there something that's wrong? Is there anything that I can do, to help you?"

She was having 'her feelings?'

"No, nothing's wrong."

"I can tell that you're upset about something? I can see it in your face. Is it something that we can talk about? If you tell me about it, will it help you to feel better?"

"I'm going upstairs to bed."

"Oh, forgive me. I didn't mean to pry?"

I ignored her because I knew what she was doing: she was asking me questions to get me started talking to her. After I was talking to her she was going to humor me and get me smiling at her, too. Then, when I was both talking and smiling, she was going ask me still more questions. It always worked for her before and I guess she thought that it would, again.

"I'm feeling good. Thank you."

"Oh, you are?"

"Yeah, I am."

"Well, good. I'm glad to hear that. But please know, my dear, that if, and when you want to talk to me about anything, I will always be here for you."

I said nothing.

She didn't either now, and I wondered why. It wasn't like her to give up easily on anything that she wanted to know. But I was glad that she was giving up. Because she was beginning to get to me. I was fighting off an urge to tell her everything.

I said nothing.

"There's barley soup cooking on the stove."

I could smell it.

"I'm going upstairs to take a nap? Call me when it's ready, okay?"

"I can do that," she said.

She picked up her book and she began to read it, again. Mary's been telling her about Jackie and me, I thought. She found out things about people without them ever knowing it. I glanced down at her as I climbed up the stairs. Her book was set aside, again. She was smiling up at me. She loves me, I thought. She's proud to have me as her son. I went up into my bedroom and I threw myself down across my bed and I stretched out as big as I could and lay as still as I could and thought about Jackie, and waited for sleep overtake me.

It wasn't much fun.

"Cortney, lunch is ready."

Mom was hollering up the stairs.

"Yeah, okay, Mom?"

"It's on the table."

"Yeah, okay. I'll be right down."

I got up and I went down into the kitchen. I sat down at the table and I filled up my bowl with the barley soup.

"Be careful, it's hot."

"What time is it?"

Mary raised her arm to look at her watch.

"It's twelve-fifteen."

I accepted the time from her, but I otherwise ignored her. I didn't like her even a little bit. I ate the barley soup and I got back up, and got back out of there.

"Thanks for the barley soup, Mom," I said, going out the door.

I walked over to the bar and I called Jackie.

"Hello."

It was her.

"Hi, Jackie. This is Cortney."

"Hi, Cortney. How are you?"

"I'm good, thank you. How about yourself?"

"I'm good too. I'm happy you called. I didn't expect you to this soon. But I'm happy you did."

"It's good to hear your voice."

"Yeah, I know. You made it home all right, eh?"

"Yeah, I did. We didn't have any trouble."

"Should I come in and see you tomorrow?"

"Yes, please do."

"Okay."

She didn't say anything.

I didn't either.

"I can't think of anything to say."

"That's alright."

"I guess I'll say goodbye."

"Okay. Bye, Cortney. I'm glad you called."

"Bye."

We both hung up.

It was the first time that we talked on the phone. I didn't realize how self-conscious I would be. But it was good to hear her voice, again. It was the first time that I heard it since she left, and it meant a lot to me.

CHAPTER 23

I WATCHED THE MOVIE SHANE AND I ATE POPCORN AND drank pop. I went upstairs to bed and I dreamt that I could fly. I swung my arms up and down and I flew up out of the yard and out over the trees. Way out high above the lake I realized that I couldn't fly. That it was some kind of a terrible mistake. I fell down towards the water and as I was about to splash down into it I woke up screaming and hollering. I dreamt it twice over and I woke up screaming and hollering each time.

My cousin Ken barged into the room. The door banged against the wall. He stuck his big hand into my face.

"Hey 'cus', put her there."

Bottom of Form

I took it and we both shook, and smiled.

"Don't squeeze my hand so goddamn hard, Ken."

He scrunched up his face and he narrowed down his eyes and smiled his big crazy grin at me. Ken wasn't my cousin at all. He was my mom's best friend's kid. We called each other cousins.

"Hey, Ken, it's good see you, again. What brings you 'Up North?'"

"Bill asked me up to do some fishing. You're coming out with us, aren't you?"

"Well, I don't know. I'll have to wait, and see."

"What does that mean, 'I'll have to wait and see?'"

"Well, he hasn't said anything to me about it. Besides, I'm working up at the resort, now. I could be working, then."

"Ha, ha. That's not what he says. He's says that you got a hot one on the line. Either that, he says, or she's got you. He says that he can't rightly tell who's got who."

"Well, Bill's been known to exaggerate a bit."

"Ha, ha. That's bullshit. He says that you're spending all your time in town, too."

"No, Ken, that's not bullshit. Jackie's not a hot one, either. She's a nice girl, and I like her a whole lot."

What the hell's wrong with Bill talking about her like that, I thought?

"Yeah sure, Cortney, if you say so?"

What the hell's wrong with them both, I thought?

"Well, actually Ken, I couldn't care less what either you or Bill think. But neither of you have any business talking about her, like that."

"Hey, cuz, loosen up a little? You're taking this way too seriously. I'm kidding with you. You're getting yourself all worked up over nothing? This is Ken here that you're talking to? Your ole buddy who's come up from the big downstate City of Flint to do some fishing with you. You don't have to hide that shit from me."

We all knew Ken best for always wanting us to level with him about everything and anything. He always thought that we were holding things back from him. But we weren't. We leveled with him about everything. But we were careful about what we said to him. His feelings were easily hurt. If we said the wrong thing to him he wouldn't talk to us for days at a time.

"If she's 'just a nice girl', then what's that big shit eating grin doing on your face. She's just a nice girl my ass, too?"

"Ken, you know us shy types don't go in for that fast stuff?"

"Ha, ha, that's bullshit, too. It's you shy types who are getting all the action, anymore.

"No, Ken, it's not bullshit. You're talking out of your asshole."

"You're the one talking out of his asshole."

"Both Bill and you are assholes."

He didn't say anything.

We stared at each other.

"This time you couldn't be more wrong, Ken."

Neither of us moved.

"Okay, Cortney, have it your own way. I didn't come up here to fight with you. I was just telling you what Bill's been telling me."

"Yeah, okay, Ken. I'm sorry."

We both smiled.

"Cortney, it's good to see you, again."

"Ken, it's good to see you again, too."

We shook hands and we both smiled, again.

"Well anyhow, what's new up here in God's Country?"

"What do you mean, 'what's new up here in God's Country?' There's actually very little that ever goes on up here?"

"Now, that I can believe. When I drove in last night I didn't see another living soul out and moving, anywhere. It's the first thing that I always notice about the place."

"Well, what do you have on the line for me, tonight?"

"What do mean, 'what do I have on the line for you?'"

"Well, I was thinking that we could get something going for later."

I thought about my plans for hitchhiking in and seeing Jackie.

"Well, I'll have to think about it."

"What does that mean, 'I'll have to think about it?'"

"Well, I was going to hitchhike in and see Jackie, later?"

"Oh, uh-huh?"

"Yeah, but now I'll have to figure out something else?"

"Well, call her up. Tell her that we'll be in later?"

"Yeah, okay? I guess I could do that?"

"What about Pam?"

"I don't know? What about her?"

"Is she still available?"

"As far as I know she is. I haven't seen her in a while."

"Well, call her up, too? Find out about her?"

"Yeah, okay? I guess I could do that, too." But I wondered why he couldn't? "Why don't you call her up? She knows you. We all went out to the movies last summer."

"Yeah, okay. I guess I could do that, eh?"

"Yeah, I think that you should."

"Well, okay then, I will."

"Good."

"What should I say to her?"

"'What do you mean, 'what should I say to her?' Ask her if she wants to go out to a movie. What else would you say?"

"I'll tell her the drive-in."

"Of course, what else?"

"You're done eating, aren't you?"

"Yeah, I am."

"Well, let's go over to the bar, and call them up."

We walked over to the bar and we called them up. We asked them if they wanted to go out to a movie. They said that they did. We played a couple games of pool and I walked back to the house and got my swimsuit. Back at the bar both Ken and I threw in for a six-pack of Budweiser. We took it out to the car and we drove up along the lake shore sipping on a cold beer and looking out through the trees at the lake. We went up across the face of the bluff and we drove through Dollar Settlement looking out at the stands of big beech trees. We went back down across the face of it and we drove back up along the lake shore looking out through the trees at the lake, again. We went through Salt Point and we drove back up across the face of the bluff and we went through Naomokong looking out at the stands of old growth Hemlock. We pulled into the overlook there and we got out and walked up to the guard rail. We stood at it and we looked out at the long rows of whitecaps racing down the lake. They were curling over in the sunlight and splashing down onto it. As I looked out at them I thought about Willis. I imagined him looking out at it and describing it by saying something like, 'grandee dandy grandee-do'. I thought about Delores. I imagined her sitting there painting the lake in all its moods. I only saw her once since I got back from Detroit. We barely said a word to each other. She was the main reason that I went off in the first place. I needed to get away from her. I stayed down there with my cousin Ken and I found a job, but I got lonely and I quit it and came back. We got back into our car and we left the overlook and drove back down across the face of the bluff. We rode back up along the lake looking out through the trees at it, again. Now that I had thought about Willis I couldn't get him off my mind. I wondered why he wasn't happy. I always thought that it was easy to be happy. That all you did was be yourself. I wondered if we would make him happy if we took him to the movies with us? Why, I wondered, were there so many unhappy kids in the goddamn world, anyway? What fucking purpose was it possibly serving?

"The goddamn mailbox is knocked off, again?"

"Huh?"

"The goddamn mailbox, it got knocked off, again."

I didn't say anything.

"It's been knocked off a hundred goddamn times, if once."

He turned into the driveway and he stopped and got out. It was lying in the grass back near the trees.

"I'll get the goddamn thing, and I'll throw it in the trunk."

He went back and he got it and he came back around and threw it in, and got back into the car.

"The nails should straighten out and I'll put it back on."

We sped up the driveway and we stopped at the cabin.

"Well, we're here," he said, looking around at the yard. "Well, nothing that I can see looks out of place. Let's go inside, and see what it looks like in there."

We got out and we went inside. I looked around at the furniture. It looked okay, too. I looked out the lakefront windows at the dock. It too looked okay. Ken sat down in a rocking chair and he rocked in it and he got back up and looked out at the dock, himself, now.

"Yeah, the dock looks okay."

He sat back down in it and as he rocked he looked around at the furniture, again. As I watched him do it, it dawned on me how much he loved the place.

"Whenever I come up here," he said, "I feel like I'm visiting with an old friend."

"Well, you are," I said, and smiled.

He smiled his big crazy grin at me.

"Well, are we going swimming, or what?"

"Yeah, of course, we are?"

"Well, let's get ready and go, then."

We went back out to the car and we got our swimsuits. We brought them in and we changed into them. We went back out and we ran down across the lawn to the beach. We ran out across it and we got out into the deep water and dived down under it. It was cold as ice. But we didn't get back up. We stayed down in it and we swam out where it was over our heads. Out there we would have to get used to it. We dived down to the bottom and we brought up flat stones and skipped across the lake. We had a contest to see who could skip theirs the farthest. He went first and he skipped his about sixty feet. I skipped mine and it went about seventy feet. I bragged to him about it and he got mad at me and began to pout. We had another contest to see who could dive under the water the farthest. He went first again and he dived under it and he swam as hard as he could for as long as he could and went about sixty feet. I dived under it and I swam as hard as I could for as long as I could and went about eighty feet. I bragged to him about it too and he got mad at me and began to pout, again. He swam back in to the beach and I swam in along behind him. We ran back up across it together and up to the cabin where we lay down in the sunlight reflecting off the lakefront windows. We drank a few beers and we warmed back up. I closed my eyes and I let my thoughts drift off and I thought about where my body quit and where the rest of the world began. I thought about its different parts: its arms, its legs, its shoulders, its head and its butt, and all the other parts of it. I caught a glimpse of my innermost feelings and I learned from them what my true feelings were about everybody and everything in my life: my Mom, my Dad, my sister, Mary, Jackie, Ellie, Willis, Ken and all the people who I worked with up at the resort. I told Ken about it and how it happened to me as I was lying in the sun and drinking a few beers and when I asked him if it ever happened to him like that, too, he said that it did. He said that when it happened to him that he always felt as if he was visiting with an old friend. Somebody who he hadn't seen for years. He scrunched up his face and he narrowed down his eyes and chuckled so hard that his whole body shook.

CHAPTER 24

KEN PULLED THE CAR UP INTO THE DRIVEWAY AND PARKED it. He got out and he walked up to the door and knocked on it. Pam opened it and, holding hands and smiling, they walked back out to it, together. I thought they were a good-looking couple. She was both slender and pretty, and dressed in polished cotton. He was both tall and handsome, and dressed in denim. He opened her door and as she got into the front seat she smiled into the back, at me.

I smiled back up at her.

"Hi, Pam. How are you?"

"I'm okay, Cortney. Thank you."

"You look good in the pant suit."

"Thank you," she said, smiling, again.

Ken closed her door for her and he walked around to his side. As he got in she slid across the seat to sit by him. They swooned as they looked in to each other's eyes. I watched them doing it until I couldn't stand to, anymore.

"It looks like love at first bite?" I said.

Pam turned around and she looked back at me.

"Cortney, you're never going to change," she said, and frowned. She turned back around and she pulled at her skirt and wriggled her butt about and got herself comfortable, again. Pam lived down the road a quarter mile from me. We went all through school, together. We used to hang out but we seldom if ever saw each other, anymore. Ken started the car and he revved it up and popped the clutch. We shot away, the tires screeching and it fish tailing. He pushed the gas pedal down to the floor and he held it and we sped off down the blacktop feeling the car shifting up through the gears, him checking for traffic, us crossing the centerline and opposing lane over onto the grass, tires pounding, rocks flying bouncing and swaying we came back out of it, him checking for traffic again, us re-crossing the opposing lane and centerline back over into our own lane and speeding off down another straight-a-way and up the hill feeling pulled down into our seat and up over the top of it feeling it fall out from under us and down through the valley and up another hill feeling pulled down into our seat and up and over the top of it, feeling it fall out from under us and speeding off down still another straight-a-way and out into the farming country to come to a screeching stop at Mackinaw Trail: we turned left onto it and we sped off in to the Soo. We drove over to the west side of it and we crisscrossed it looking for her house. We couldn't find it and we pulled into a gas station and asked for directions to it and, boom, drove right over to it.

It was a long narrow two-story setting out by the side walk.

"Halleluiah! Praise the Lord," said Ken, throwing his arms into the air. "We're here at long last!"

The rest of us looked around at each other, and smiled.

I got out and I walked up to the door and rang the doorbell. Nobody answered it and I looked back at them.

"Now what?"

"Try knocking on it? No wait. Go back around the side. There's a driveway that goes back in?"

I walked around the side of the house. The driveway went in to a back porch. There were flowers growing around it. As I climbed the steps I smelled them. They were pretty, but they actually stunk.

I knocked on the door.

She opened it. "Hi, Cortney," she said.

We both smiled.

"Hi, Jackie. How are you, today?"

We kissed and hugged.

"It's good to see you, again."

"It's good to see you, again, too," I said.

She stepped back with the door and I walked by her into the kitchen. I stood and I looked around at it. I wasn't looking to be critical, but I noticed that the walls were dirty. That they needed to be cleaned, or painted or something.

"So, this is where you live, eh?"

She didn't say anything.

I sensed that she wanted me to like it.

"You have a nice place, here," I said.

"Thank you," she said.

As she said it her tooth moved, again. I ignored it and I went on with my thoughts.

But, before I could say anything else, she said, "I still have these curlers to take out."

She put her hands up into her hair.

"Sure, okay. Take your time. The drive-in won't open for quite a while, yet."

"Dad's in the living room. You can wait in there with him, if you want to."

"Thanks, I think I will."

"Good. I'll hurry, and take these out."

She walked out through an open doorway into a stairwell. I walked out through a hallway into the living room.

Armand looked up at me.

"Hi, Cortney. Come in and sit down."

"Thank you."

He moved over on the couch for me. I went in and I sat down by him.

"How are you, today?" I said.

"I'm good, thank you. How about yourself?"

"Oh, I'm good, too."

Willis was bouncing in a chair.

"Hi, Willis. How are you?"

He ignored me.

"Willis, say 'hi' to Cortney. He said 'hi' to you."

He ignored his dad, too.

"You found our house, alright, eh?"

"Yeah, we did. We stopped at the gas station, and asked directions to it."

He looked at Willis.

"Willis, Cortney is here visiting with us. We have to be nice to him?"

He ignored his dad, again.

"This summer's been a hot one, eh?"

"Yeah, it has. One of our hottest, ever."

We both looked at the TV.

There was a stern look on his face when I looked back at him. He was thinking seriously about something.

"I don't know what gets into him, sometimes," he said. "We taught him to have better manners than that."

"Oh, he's okay. He's still a little boy?"

"Yeah, I guess so? Maybe that's it, eh? Say, when you stopped in I was watching this here National Geographic Special. It's about these dolphins on here and how smart they really are. These two scientists seem to think that they're as smart as the monkeys are, and maybe even more so."

"Yeah, I read something about that?"

"Yeah, they're doing a lot of research on them. Now they seem to think that they have their own way of talking." He stopped, and he looked at me, to see if I understood him. "You know, talking back and forth to each other, the way we are, now."

"Oh really? I haven't heard that, before?"

"Oh, yeah? Someday, they're going find out how smart they really are?"

"Yeah, that should be interesting, eh?"

"Yeah, it should. I like watching these National Geographic Specials. I learn something new about things whenever I do."

"Yeah, I do, too."

Jackie walked into the room.

"I'm ready to go."

I got up, to go out with her.

"Take care, Armand. We'll talk to you again later, okay?"

"Yeah, okay, Cortney. You two have your selves a good time."

"Thank you."

As I walked pass Willis he glanced up at me. I thought better of saying anything to him. Jackie and I went out the door, together. We held hands and we walked out to the car.

I opened her door for her.

Pam looked out it. "Hi, Jackie, I'm Pam. How are you?"

"I'm good. Thank you, Pam."

They both shook hands, and smiled.

Ken looked in to the back at her. "I'm Ken, Jackie. How are you?"

"I'm good, Ken. Thank you?"

They both shook hands, and smiled, now, too.

I noticed him giving her the once-over.

"Now, I can see why Cortney likes you so much," he said.

Jackie's face turn red.

Ken revved up the car and he popped the clutch and shot away, the tires screeching and it fish tailing, again.

"Ken, Jackie's Dad is inside the door?"

"Hey bro, which way?"

"Take a left here, and go straight across town."

"Hey bro, I got yah," he said, and smiled.

We turned off onto Spruce Street. We drove through the historic district looking out at the big ornate homes built when lumber was cheap. We wondered what it was like to live in them. We went into the business district and we drove through it and back out to the big ornate homes. We stayed on Spruce all the way out to Sherman Park. We pulled into the parking lot and we parked and walked up to the gate. We paid at it and we went inside and walked up the causeway, together. We stopped at the first tent and we played a game of ring toss and when I won a stuffed lion and gave it to Jackie she got all excited about it. She hugged it and me and then it, again. It was the same lion as the one on the cover of the album, The Lion Sleeps Tonight. Its title song was also her favorite song. We walked further up the causeway, together. We stopped at the tent with the milk jugs sitting on the top of the milk can. We played a game and Ken knocked them all off with the baseballs and when he won a stuffed bear and he gave it to Pam she got all excited about it, too. Like Jackie, she hugged it and him and then it, again. I told her that it looked like her and she made a face at me. We walked still further up the causeway, together. We stopped at the tent with the wheel of fortune game in it. We each put a dollar down on the red squares and when the woman spun the wheel and it stopped on the blue square we each lost our dollar. The rides all cost too much, and we didn't go on any of them. We walked back down the causeway, together. We went back out the gate and we walked back out to the car and got back into it. We got back out onto Spruce and we drove back out to Baker Side Road and turned off onto it. We drove out it to the Dondee Bowling Alley on the edge of town and we pulled into it. We parked the car and we got out and went inside. We rented shoes and we got bowling balls and we found a lane and bowled a game of it.

By the end of it my bowling hand was tired.

"Anybody for another game?" I said.

Nobody said anything.

"My bowling hand is too tired."

I held it up for them to see.

Nobody bothered to look at it. They were putting their bowling balls away.

"Well, I'm ready, if you guys are."

Nobody said anything.

"We can go for a ride out into the country, if you want to? The drive-in won't open for another hour or so."

Nobody said anything.

They were busy changing their shoes, now.

Ken took Pam's hand.

"Hey, bro, we're out of here," he said.

I took Jackie's hand and we followed them back out the door. We walked back out to the car and we got back into it and got back out onto Baker Side Road. We drove out into the country and we turned off onto a gravel road and Ken revved up the car and he popped the clutch and shot away, the tires spinning and it fish tailing and throwing up a cloud of dust now. Tractors were out in the hayfields along it pulling big haying machines cutting, raking and rolling the hay up into round bails. Other tractors were coming along behind it pulling big wrapping machines and wrapping them in white plastic for hauling off and lining up along the fences. We thought they looked like giant marshmallows. In other fields cows plodded their way back to their barns. We stopped an intersection and we turned off onto another gravel road and went speeding off on it, the tires spinning and it fish-tailing and throwing up another cloud of dust. Out along it in the hayfields other big haying operations were going on. Pam looked out her window and she saw that the western sky was on fire. She said something to us about it and we looked out at it and Ken stopped the car. He turned it around and he revved up the motor and popped the clutch and we sped back in to town, the tires spinning and it fish-tailing and throwing up yet another cloud of dust.

"Hey, bro," said Ken, throwing up his arms, "we're out of here! Like shit from a monkey's asshole."

The rest of us looked around at each other, and smiled, again.

Back in town we drove over to the drive-in theater and we paid at the gate and went through to the back. We parked and we got out and walked up to the refreshment stand and bought popcorn and pop. We took them back to the car with us and we snacked on them as we watched the cartoons. The movie started and Ken's arm went up and around Pam's shoulders and she move over close to him. I put my arm up and around Jackie's shoulders and she moved over close to me, now, too.

We settled in to watch the movie, like that.

But Jackie and I couldn't see over back of the front seat. We could barely see the top half of the movie. We watched it like that but then we quit and from the sounds of it in the front seat both Ken and Pam did, too. We could hear them squirming about and kissing and hugging. I scooted ahead on our seat and I turned around and kissed Jackie on the lips. I kissed her ears, her eyes, her cheeks, and her nose. I recited a love poem to her. She liked it so much that I recited another one to her and she liked it so much too that I recited still another one and I kept on reciting them to her until the movie got over. The lights came back on and I got back around on the seat by Jackie and Pam slid across her seat and rolled her window down and reached out and hung up the speaker and Ken started the car and it began to move. We got back out onto Baker Side Road and we drove back out into the country and turned off onto another gravel road. We sped off down it listening to Elvis Presley singing 'Love Me Tender' and watching as the road unfurled in the car lights ahead of us barely in time for it to hurl down it.

I whispered to Jackie.

"I love you, Jackie," I said.

She was quiet beside me.

"Do you have something to tell me?"

"I love you, too," she said.

Well, I thought, she finally said it to me. It felt good hearing it. But I felt too that I should have waited for her to say it to me on her own. I felt that it would have meant even more to me.

CHAPTER 25

"CORTNEY, LUNCH IS READY."

Mom was hollering up the stairs.

"Yeah, okay, Mom. I'll be right down."

I got up out of bed and I pulled on my trousers and went down into the kitchen. It was after twelve, already. The show got over at two. I sat down at the table and I filled up my bowl with the barley soup. I blew on it to cool it off and I ate it and got back up. I went out the door and I walked out through the yard to the black-top and started down it. I got down past the fishery before a car stopped and picked me up. It took me in to the Soo and it dropped me off downtown.

I walked out to her place.

As I knocked on the door she opened it. We kissed and hugged and said hello. She stepped back with it and I walked by her into the kitchen.

She followed me into it.

"How are you, today?"

"I'm okay, thanks."

Willis ran in from the living room.

"Hi, Cortney. How are you?"

"I'm okay. Thank you, Willis. How about yourself?"

He ignored me and he ran back into it. I looked behind him and someone's feet were propped up onto a footstool. I wanted to kiss Jackie but I didn't want anybody to see me. I stepped back and I leaned back on the refrigerator, and pulled her to me. She leaned in against me with the whole length of her body on mine.

We kissed and hugged, like that.

"Do you want to go for a walk?"

"Sure, where to?"

"I have another favorite place to show you. Would you like to see it?"

"Yeah, I would, very much so."

"Or, you could show me one of yours, instead?"

She didn't say anything.

"It's your turn to, if you want to?"

"I don't have any."

"Not any, at all?"

"No, not any at all?"

"Well, let's go for walk then, and see where we end up?"

We went out the door into the street. There weren't any cars in it. We walked up the middle of it. I looked out across a field of cattails. I saw what looked like a football stadium.

I pointed to it.

"Is that a football stadium over there?"

She looked out at it. "Yeah, that's the Athletic Field."

"If you want to, we can walk over to it?"

"Yeah, okay."

"We can cut through those cattails, if you want to?"

She looked out at them.

"Yeah, that's a good idea," she said.

We went over to the cattails and we walked into them. There was a yellow dead look to them. The ground under them was black. It looked like it got muddy in the rain. We pushed our way through them and we came to a trail and turned off onto it. It narrowed down and then faded and disappeared, altogether. We pushed our way through them again and we came to another trail and turned off onto it, too. It also narrowed down and then faded and disappeared, altogether. We pushed our way through them still again and when we didn't come to another trail we stopped and looked around ourselves. We didn't see another trail and I reached out for her and she came into my arms. She leaned in against me and we kissed and hugged like that and then we knelt down onto our knees and rolled over onto our sides, hearing the cattail crumple under us, kissed and hugged there and rolled onto our backs, hearing cattail crumple under us again, and lay there holding hands and looking up through their stalks at the sky. We looked to either side of us. The stalks were thick where they came up out of the bare black earth. I kissed and hugged her again and I got on top of her and when I began to take off my clothes and she didn't, I stopped. I began to put them back on but worried that I could miss out on doing it to her, I stopped again. I began to take them back off, again.

"Can I do it to you?"

She didn't say anything.

I got back off her and I put my clothes back on.

"It's really quiet in here, eh?"

She didn't say anything.

"Jackie, you're a good-looking girl."

"Thank you."

We both smiled a little.

"You're perfect in every way, your body, your clothes, how you walk, everything about you."

"Thank you."

"You have a pretty smile, too."

She blushed a little.

"What's the name of your haircut?"

"It's called a pixie."

"It looks good on you."

"Thank you."

"It feels like we're laying down out in the country some-where, eh?"

"Yeah, it does."

I kissed her hand.

"It's really nice in here, eh?"

She didn't say anything.

I kissed her other hand.

"I love your freckles, too."

"Thank you," she said, again.

I scooted around sideways to her. I put my head in her lap. I went to sleep and when I woke back up she was sleeping, too. I woke her up and she sat up and pushed the hair out of her face.

"We both took a little snooze."

She rubbed her eyes.

"I didn't realize I was so tired."

"I didn't realize I was, either," I said.

"You don't have a lot to say about things, do you? Is it that you like to be quiet? Or that you don't have a lot to say?"

She didn't say anything.

"I don't mean to say that there's anything wrong with it? It's just something that I noticed about you."

She didn't say anything.

"It's not something that I don't like about you, either. I like everything about you."

She said nothing.

"Jackie, do you truly love me?"

She looked in to my eyes.

"Yes, Cortney, I do truly love you, very much so."

"Good. I truly love you, too."

I got on top of her and when I went to touch her I remembered what my sister said: she said that you loved someone for who they were and not for what you could get from them. I didn't fully understand what she meant at the time. But after what happened to Delores and me, I did now.

I got back off her.

"Are you ready to go?"

"Yeah, if you are, I am?"

"Yeah, I am," I said.

We got up and we pushed through the cattail, again. We came to another trail and we turned off onto it. We followed it out onto the athletic field. We stood, and we looked around ourselves. The City Garage was off to our right. The football stadium was across the playing field. We walked out to it and we crossed it and climbed up the bleachers. We sat down at the top and we looked back down at it. I remembered a track meet that I went to there.

"Did you ever go to a track meet here?"

"No, I didn't."

"Oh, that's too bad. Our school competed in the invitational's here. If you would have, you might have seen me."

"Oh, really?"

"Yeah, I ran the mile in them."

"Oh uh-huh? How did you do?"

"Actually, I didn't do very good. I didn't even finish most of the races."

"Oh, how come?"

"Well, the other runners were fast starters. I wore myself out trying to keep up to them. By the end of the race I was so far behind everybody else that I quit, and walked off the track."

"Oh, that's too bad."

"Yeah, it is. But I guess that's how it goes. You either have to train hard and then run your own race, or else you lose."

She didn't say anything.

I wondered if I sounded really smart?

"Did I sound really smart to you?"

"Well, you are really smart?"

"Do you like smart people?"

"Oh, I don't know? What do you mean by smart people?"

"Well, I guess, people who know a lot about things?"

"I haven't actually thought about it."

"Well, sometimes I think that I act smarter than I actually am? I'm actually a very average person."

She didn't say anything.

"Well, if you didn't go to the track meets here, then I guess you didn't see me here."

"No, I guess not? Are you hungry?"

"Yeah, I am, a little."

"We should get started back. Mom's probably got supper on, by now."

"Yeah, okay."

We both got up.

We walked back down the bleachers, together. We walked back across the playing field. We went back in to the cattail. We followed the same trail and when it too narrowed down and then faded and disappeared, altogether, we pushed through them and when we came to another trail we turned off onto it. When it didn't narrow down and then fade and disappear, altogether, we walked back through on it. We came back out onto the street and, still no cars in it, we walked back up the middle of it. We got back to her house and when she opened the door to go inside I took a half step back. She didn't think to invite me in to eat with them. I felt that if I were to go in now, it would be like I was inviting myself in.

I took another half step back.

"I'm think I'm going downtown, and eat."

She didn't say anything.

"I'll come back, later, after I do, okay?"

She still didn't say anything.

I turned and as I walked away I heard her take a big breath behind me. I slowed back down but when I heard the door close as she went inside, I sped back up, again.

CHAPTER 26

I WALKED DOWNTOWN TO FRANK'S PLACE. I WENT INTO IT and I sat down at a booth in the front windows. I ordered a cup of coffee and a hamburger and as I waited for it I watched the cars go by. The waitress brought it out to me and I ate the hamburger and drank off my coffee. I got back up and I paid for it on the way back out. I walked back down Portage to Barbeau and I turned off onto it and walked over to her house. I went into it and she was in the kitchen washing dishes.

I stood by her and we chatted.

"Is it hot out, today?"

"Yeah, it is."

"It will probably be cooler inside, today. We can stay here and watch tv, if you want to."

"Yeah, okay."

We walked out into the living room. We sat down on the couch and we turned on the tv and watched an old Western.

Willis was bouncing in his chair.

"Willis, we can't hear the tv. Will you please stop that bouncing?"

He ignored her.

He was staring at the wall ahead. I looked in to see what was on it. There was nothing on it. I looked off into Armand's bedroom and he was asleep in his bed. I wondered where Bunny was.

"Where's your mother at, Jackie?"

Her face turned red.

"She went out to the bar."

"Oh really?"

"Yeah, she picked a fight with dad to have an excuse to go. She used to go out on the weekends. But now she goes out whenever she can get away from him."

"Oh, that's too bad?"

"Yeah, it is."

"Doesn't your dad drink?"

"No, he doesn't. Just my Mom does."

"It's usually the other way around, eh?"

"Yeah, it usually is," she said.

Her face got red, again.

I changed the subject.

"What's the name of this old Western"

"I'm not sure. But I think it's Gun Smoke. Matt Dillon was on." Dillon came on, again. "See, it was him."

I didn't say anything.

Willis was still bouncing in his chair.

"Willis, we can't hear the tv. Please stop that bouncing?"

He ignored her, again. Two cowboys were beating up on Dillon. Festus arrived and helped him out. Together, they beat up on the cowboys. They arrested them, and they hustled them off to jail. Later when a lynch mob gathered out front they snuck them out the back door and over to the next county where they would be safe and get a fair trial. Love Has Many Faces came on next. After it, Mission Impossible and after it we got back up and walked out to the door, together. Outside it, we kissed and hugged out in the silvery moonlight and we said goodnight.

She went back inside, and I struck off for home.

I was going to hitchhike back home to get a good night's sleep in my bed. I was going to get up in the morning and hitchhike back to town. But now it was too late to do it. I would get there and get into bed and I would have to get back up and hitchhike back to town. I remember when my Dad got stuck in town overnight, what he did. He walked over to the city jail and he asked them if he could sleep in an empty cell. They always let him do it. So, I decided to do that, too.

Tonight, the water puddles were back in the streets. I walked around them, and I kept my shoes dry. The porch lights were reflecting in them again and lighting up the neighborhoods a little. Tonight, the patches of fog were back in the streets, too. Were it not for the lone police cruiser out patrolling them there would have been another living soul out anywhere. I got down to the city jail and I rang the night buzzer and waited for the door to click. It clicked, and I opened it and went inside. I walked down a corridor and I stopped at the Sheriff's Office. I waited at the window for the officer on duty to get up from behind his desk.

He got up from it and he walked over to me.

"Can I help you with something?"

"Yeah, I'm looking for a place to sleep?"

"Oh?"

"Yeah, I was wondering if I could sleep in an empty cell."

He handed a pencil to me. He looked down at the ledger on the counter. He took it in both hands and he gave it a spin.

We both waited for it to stop.

He stuck his finger down on the line.

"Sign there," he said.

I signed it where he wanted me to. He went out through an open doorway. He came out from around the corner carrying a big ring of keys. He walked by me without looking.

"This way," he said.

I followed him back up the corridor. We went out through a set of steel doors. We walked up the next corridor, together. There were cells along the sides of it. There were dark shadows of steel bars on the walls. The prisoners were sleeping in them with dark gray blankets pulled up tightly around their necks. We stopped at an empty cell and he opened it and I walked into it. I looked around it as he locked it back up behind me.

"Somebody will get you up at six," he said. He walked back up the corridor.

The cell wasn't dirty, but it wasn't clean, either. The beds, the stool, the ceiling, everything in it was painted the dark gray. The single naked light bulb in the center of the ceiling reflected off wherever it was worn bare. The bunks didn't have mattresses on them? What, I thought, no mattresses on the bunks? I looked in to the cells to either side of mine. There were mattresses on the bunks. The son of a bitch put me into a cell without mattresses on the bunks, I thought. He did it on purpose, too. I lied down to see how it would feel without a mattress. It felt like I was lying down on a slab of concrete. I got back up and I walked across to the corridor.

`I pushed my head in against the bars.

"You fuckin' no-good son of a bitchin' bastard."

"Hey, Mister, quiet down over there."

I quieted back down. I sensed that whoever said it meant it. I didn't want the guard to come back and to throw me back out into the street, either. I would be back out in them again with nowhere to sleep. I walked back across to the bunks and I lied down and I squirmed about and got as comfortable as I could and went off to sleep. I slept through the whole night without waking back up. I woke up in the morning to the sound of footsteps coming down the corridor. I got up and I walked across to the bars and pushed my head in against them, again. There was a guard walking down it. He wasn't the one who locked me up. He stopped when he got down to my cell and he unlocked it and opened it. I walked out into the corridor and I waited as he locked it back up. We walked back up the corridor, together. I didn't mention anything about the bunks. I figured he wouldn't know anything about it. We went out through the steel doors and we walked back up the next corridor and as we came up on the door that I came into last night I hurried off ahead of him and went back out it and, boom, I was back out in the street. Wow, did it feel good.

I struck off for Frank's Place.

I went into it and I sat down at the booth in the front windows. I ordered a cup of coffee and as I waited for it I watched the other customers eat their breakfast. They finished them, and they got back up and paid for them on the back way out. The waiter hurried back out to the tables and they picked up their tips and put the dirty dishes onto a busing cart. They reset the tables and they hurried back into the kitchen with them. The customers waiting up at the cashier walked out to them and sat down. The waiters hurried back out to them and they took their orders and went back into the kitchen, again. Shortly they came back out of it carrying hot pots of coffee. Later they came back out of it carrying hot plates of food. They took them over to the tables and they sat them down in front of the customers. They refilled their cups of coffee and they went back into the kitchen, again. Now my waiter brought out my hot cup of coffee out to me. She sat it down in front of me and she went back into the kitchen, herself, now. I drank it and I got up and paid for it on the way back out, too. I walked back over to Ashmun and I turned off onto it and walked down it to Water Street. I turned off onto it and I walked down it to Kemp's Coal Dock and sat down on their wharf. I watched the sun come up out of the river. It looked like a big ball of fire was coming up out of it. The whole harbor was lighted up. I got back up and I walked back out to Portage and I turned off onto it and walked down to Barbeau. I turned off onto it and I walked over to Jackie's and rang the doorbell. She answered the door wearing her pajamas. There was a Mickey Mouse picture on them. I tried not to smile at her but I couldn't help myself.

I smiled at her.

"I know. They look funny on me, don't they?"

I didn't say anything.

"That's okay. You can smile at me, if you want. My Mom got them for me as a Christmas present. She meant them as a joke. I only wear them when nothing else is clean."

"I'm sorry. But they do look funny on you."

"Yeah, I know they do."

"But in a cute sort of way?" I said.

"Thank you," she said, and smiled.

We both smiled, now.

I noticed something else about her. Actually, I noticed it about her before. Whenever she said thank you to me her front tooth moved. It sounded more like she was saying, 'tank you.' Back then I wasn't ready to accept that about her. But I was now: she wore a false tooth. It moved when she said, 'thank you' to you, sometimes.

CHAPTER 27

BUNNY WALKED INTO THE ROOM.

"Hi, Cortney. How are you, today?"

"I'm good, Bunny. Thank you."

She poured herself a cup of coffee.

"Cortney, do you drink coffee?"

"Yeah, I do."

"Would you like a cup?"

"No, I had one downtown. But thanks for asking me."

"You're welcome. Would you like to have another one? Or, maybe it's too soon?"

"Yeah, it's too soon. Thank you."

She sat down at the table. She pointed down it at a chair."

"You can sit down there."

"Thank you."

I sat down in it.

"Did you have breakfast?"

"Yeah, I did," I said, and lied. "I ate downtown."

"Are you sure?"

"Yeah," I said and lied, again. "But thanks for asking."

"What's the weather like outside?" Jackie said.

"It's really nice out."

"Good. I'll get dressed and we can go for a walk, if you want to?"

"Yeah, I do. That's a good idea."

"My God, Jackie, Cortney and I are talking? You butt in, and you take right over?"

"I just asked him a question, Mom?"

"Well, maybe he doesn't want to go for a walk with you. Maybe he wants to stay here and talk to me. Did you even think of that? Before you so rudely butted in, and took over?"

Jackie left for the stairs.

"She's my daughter and I love her to death. But sometimes I can't stand her. She only thinks of herself."

I didn't say anything.

"I'm sorry for the way this place looks this morning. It hasn't been picked up, yet. That kid of mine, she could stay here and help me. But is she going to? Oh no, not her. Are you kidding me?" She puffed at her cigarette. "No, she's going to run off somewhere and leave it for her mother to do." She blew her smoke at the ceiling fan. "I guess that's all I'm supposed to be good for around here, is picking up behind them?" It swirled around it and it slowly disappeared. "She told you that I was out drinking last night, didn't she?"

"No," I said, and lied still again.

"Things would be better around here if they helped me with things. But none of them will. Not one of them. But they all want me to be right here for them. I can't go out anywhere without hearing about it. They're worried that I'll go out and have a good time without them. If they appreciated me around here, it would be different. But they don't. Not one of them does." She puffed at her cigarette. "Your mother goes out and has a good time, doesn't she?"

"Yeah, she does."

"Why of course, she does? You need to. You go crazy sitting around the house all the time by yourself. When you get back you appreciate more of what you have, too."

I didn't say anything.

"They make out around here like I'm a bad person of some kind. Just because I like to go out alone to the bars in the evenings." She drank of her coffee. "She told you that her dad doesn't drink, eh? That I'm the drinker in this house?"

"No," I said, and lied yet again.

Jackie walked back into the room.

"I'm ready to go."

I got up to go out with her.

"I enjoyed talking to you, Bunny," I said, still lying.

"Cortney, I enjoyed talking to you, too. We'll talk again later, okay?"

"Yeah, okay."

We both smiled.

Jackie and I went out the door. We struck off up the street, together.

"Did she start in on you?"

"Yeah, she did."

"I thought that she would. I'm sorry for leaving you alone with her."

"That's okay."

"She's terrible when she has a hangover. I didn't want her to start in on me. That's why I walked right through to the door. I'm glad that she didn't. Because I don't think that I would have held myself back, today. And, if I say anything at all to her, it only makes matters worse."

"Yeah, it's best to just get along, sometimes."

"Yeah, it is. But the problem with her is, she usually doesn't want to."

We turned off onto Portage.

"It feels good to be off by ourselves again, eh?"

"Yeah, it sure does. It feels really good?"

"You forget how good, eh?"

"Yeah, you do?"

"Well, where are we off to?"

"I don't know? Any place is okay by me?"

"Well, let's walk down to the river, then. I sat down on Kemp's Coal Dock on the way over. I watched the sun coming up out of the river. It looked like a big ball of fire was coming up out of it. The whole harbor was lighted up."

"I wish I was there with you."

"Yeah, I wish that you were, too. It was really something to see."

"Did you make it home, alright?"

"No, actually, I didn't."

"Oh, really? Where'd you sleep?"

"I slept in the city jail...

"Oh, really? How come down there?"

"Well, there wasn't enough time to hitchhike home and back. And, I remembered what my dad did when he got stuck in town overnight. He walked over to the city jail and he asked them if he could sleep in an empty cell. They always let him do it. So, I did that, too. But the guard put me into one without mattresses on the bunks. I slept on a hard sheet of steel."

"They wouldn't put you into a cell with mattresses on them?"

"Well, I didn't ask them to. I just thought that they would. I didn't realize what he did until after he left. I felt like I didn't have a say in the matter. That it was either that or nothing. So, I lied down on it and I made the most of it."

"It's hard to understand why they'd be so mean to you?"

"Yeah it is? But anyhow, I'm still tired and I'm sore all over now too and I'm hoping that we can walk up along the river somewhere and find a place to lie down on some good ole green grass and stretch out really big in the warm sun and take a little snooze in it and relax and soak it up and lull the day away."

CHAPTER 28

WE WALKED UP ALONG THE RIVER. WE CAME TO A LAWN with a few trees on it. We walked over to one and we laid down under it. The shipping canal was barely thirty feet away from us, now. We watched a ship come up it. It turned in to the pier and it eased itself in against it. It rubbed on the fender timbers as it came up it toward us. Smoke rose up from them as it went by us and in behind a big government-looking building.

"They sure are long, eh?"

"Yeah, they sure are."

"Have you been here, before?"

"No, I haven't."

"I haven't, either. It's funny considering how close we live, eh?"

"Yeah, it is. Can I put my head in your lap?"

"Yeah, sure," she said.

She sat up with her back against the tree. I got around sideways to her and I put my head in it. There was a chain-length fence around both the big government looking building and the lawn. There was barbed wire along the top of them. There was an official look about the whole place. If it weren't for the Veteran's Memorial out at the gate we wouldn't have come through it. We watched another ship come up the canal. It turned into the pier and it eased itself in against it, too. It rubbed the fender timbers as it came up it. Smoke rose up from them as it went by us and in behind the big government-looking building, too.

I recited a poem to her.

> The Red Man's Red Earth
> The long red ship, long hauling,
> The red man's iron earth,
> Off to the factories of war,

For building the Air Force Predators,
And Global Hawks,
The red man's red earth,
Bulging in its holds,
Sailing towards a red sky,
In the morning,
A sailor's warning,
To bound the hatches,
And, cover the moorings.

A ship loaded out with iron ore was on its way down across Lake Superior. It was going down through the Soo Locks into the Ste. Marys Fall's Canal. Down through it and out across Lake Huron into Lake St. Clair and the Detroit River and all the defense factories located along it.

I recited a Dylan Thomas poem to her.

Do Not Go Gentle Into That Good Night
Do not go gentle into that good-night,
Old age should burn and rave at close of day;
Rage, rage against the dying of the light.
Though wise men at their end know dark is right,
Because their words had forked no lightning they
Do not go gentle into that good night.

There were four more stanzas to it. But I couldn't remember all the words to them. So, I stopped there.

She smiled at me.

"That's a great poem. I really like it."

"It's one of my favorites."

"How did you ever remember it?"

"If you like them, they're easy to remember."

"I haven't remembered any."

"Until I took a poetry class, I didn't, either. But since taking it I've remembered lots of them. We had to do it for class and I learned to like it."

"I think you have a talent for it."

"Thank you."

She didn't say anything.

"Some poems I've remembered for just when I'm off alone with a pretty girl."

She blushed a little.

"I can be a goofball, sometimes, eh?"

"Yeah, you can. But, I like that about you, too."

We watched another ship come up the canal. It turned into the pier and it eased itself in against it, too. It also rubbed on the fender timbers as it came up it. Smoke rose up from them as it went by us and in behind the big government-looking building, too. There was a lone sailor standing out at the deck winch. He gave a cat call when he saw us. I kissed Jackie and I waved to him and the smile left his face. The poor son of a gun is stuck out there alone on that ship, I thought, away from all those he loves. I thought of another poem to recite. It was about a girl mourning the loss of her lover. I recited it and then part of an ode about an old man that went blind later in life and who could no longer see the places of his youth.

Ode to Immortality

Then, sing, ye birds, sing, sing a joyous song!
Be now forever taken from my sight.
Though nothing can bring back the hour
Of splendour in the grass, of glory in the flower;
We will grieve not, rather find
Strength in what remains behind.

I always felt good after I recited it. I asked her if she felt good, too, and she said that she did. I rolled down off her lap and I pulled her down onto the grass with me. We lay beside each other holding hands and looking up through the branches at the sky. It went out away and off into forever. We looked up at the homes on the slopes above Soo, Ontario. They looked big out in the bright sun.

We looked closer-by at the Saint Marys' Rapids. They looked small with the five navigation locks, three power houses, two bridges and the row of compensating gates built on them. We tried to imagine the surprised look on white men's faces when they saw them for the first time. We talked about the ships coming from all over the world and using the locks to go up into Lake Superior. We talked about all the countries with atomic bombs and wondered if they would use them in another war. We talked about watching the doomsday scenarios on TV and realizing for the first time how dangerous it was to live here on earth. We talked about sending a man to Mars and wondered if it was even possible to go to Mars. I went on alone from there: I told her about all the things that happened to me. About all the things that I still hoped to do. About all the places where I still hoped to travel before I died. I told her what I thought about the world wasting so much of its wealth on wars: how instead we all could be living in new houses. I told her about the things that I did up until then that I never told another living human being: how I could lay on the beach and I could drink a few beers and glimpse my innermost feelings and learn from them what my true feelings were about everybody and everything in my life. And, as we lay there talking and holding hands and looking up through the branches at the sky she listened to me like nobody before or since and although I thought that she should tire of it she didn't tire of it and she listened to me as if every word that I said was important to her. Snuggling up on the grass in the sunlight with all our lovely afternoons melting into one time itself seemed to stop and go away and as we gave ourselves over to the day there was nothing else but us and the broad sweep of the lawn and the lazy flow of the river and the summer blue sky and the warm gentle breeze wafting across the lawn and over our bodies. When her body called out to mine I reached out for her and I felt of her face and I went down onto her neck and down onto her breasts and further down onto her stomach and in between her legs to where I felt of her what I always wanted to feel of a pretty girl. I got on top of her and I moved on her like I was doing it to her and as I got back off her I moved away from her to where I look back at her and see the Jackie that I loved: the pretty girl wearing the white blouse over the firm breasts, the polished cotton tan capris covering the slender legs, the round eyes squinting against the sunlight and the painful look in them and, when I moved back over by her and I lay back down by her with only our arms touching, it was enough. The moms and dads walked by with their kids and they looked down at us and we looked back up at them and saw enough of ourselves to snuggle up still closer and to kiss and hug still harder and to know in our hearts that we would always be together.

"I'm hungry? What about you?"

"Yeah, I am, too."

"It must be after five, by now?"

"Yeah, I think it is."

"We can eat uptown, today, if you want to?"

"Yeah, okay," she said.

I seldom if ever ate in a restaurant as I was growing up. My folks were the kind who went to town and got whatever it was they needed and got back out. They seldom if ever ate in a restaurant when I went in with them. But after I got a job and I had my own money I ate in them as often as I could. I always felt as if I was living on high whenever I did.

There are thirty some restaurants in the Soo. It's a lot for a town its size. But it's a tourist town and the people who live in it make their living off them. There used to be a tannery, a woolen mill and a carbide factory. But they all shut down after they couldn't make a profit, anymore.

My Dad spoke out about things that bothered him. He thought that the City fathers were trying to take Whitefish Bay away from the commercial fishermen and give it to the sportsmen. He got angry when he talked about it. He always wanted it to be there for his family and himself when times were hard.

"Where should we eat?"

"Sometimes Ellie and I ate lunch up at the Delmar. We could walk up there, and eat, if you want to."

"Yeah, okay. That sounds good."

We walked up across the lawn and we went out the gate and walked on Portage over to Ashmun. We turned off onto it and we walked up to the Delmar looking out at the tourists driving by in their big SUVs and trucks. In the summer hundreds of thousands of them come 'up north' to visit the World Famous, Soo Locks in the summer. They buy fudge in the fudge shops and they walk the gyp-strip shoving it into their mouths. They wear bright shirts and shorts and turn their hats around backward and prop up their sunglasses on them. The Soo Locks is the only place around for hundreds of miles where they can get up close enough to a big ship to actually touch it.

We went into the Delmar and walked through to the back. We sat down in a booth and I took out my wallet and counted my money. There were four dollars in it. I searched into my pockets and I found six coins. I added them up and now there was four dollars and sixty-six cents.

I searched into my pockets, again.

"Cortney, is something wrong?"

"Huh?"

"Is something wrong?"

"No, it's okay."

I saw the waitress walking back.

"I'm a little short of money, today, Jackie. Is it alright if you have a hamburger and I don't, and we both get a cup of coffee?"

The waitress stopped at our booth.

"One hamburger, please. Jackie, do you want the works on it?"

She didn't say anything.

"The works on it, please, and two cups of coffee."

The waitress repeated our order back to us. I nodded and she smiled, and left.

"Cortney, aren't you hungry?"

"No," I said, and lied.

She didn't say anything.

We sat quietly waiting for our order.

The waitress brought our order out to us. Jackie picked up her hamburger and took a bite of it. She looked across the booth at me. I looked back across it at her. Neither of us said anything. She finished eating it and we drank off our coffees and we got back up and got back out of there. We both felt better walking outside in the sunlight. We walked back down Ashmun to Portage. When I checked for traffic I noticed the gate into the Soo Locks. I asked her if she ever saw the locks and she said that she didn't. I didn't see them, either. I asked her if she wanted to go and see them, and she said that she did. We walked up Portage and we went in through the gate and walked up the sidewalk to the observation platform. We climbed up the stairs and we stood on it and looked out at the ships. Two of them were in the locks. Both were locking upbound to the lake head. The sailor who we saw standing out at the deck winch earlier was still standing out at it. I waved to him and he waved back to me. The man standing next to me hollered out to him.

"Sir, what you loaded out with?"

"Chickens."

"Where are you bound out for, sir?"

"Australia."

"Thank you, sir. Good sailing to you, sir."

He waved to the sailor, but the sailor didn't wave back. He was walking up the deck smiling now a hugely wise grin. The fudgy reported back to his wife and kids on what he learned.

"Some wise guy, eh?"

"Yeah, that's for sure."

"Well, have you seen enough of the World Famous, Soo Locks?"

She both nodded, and smiled.

"Well, let's get out of here, then?"

We walked back down the stairs, together.

"Where are we off to now, back to our tree?"

"Yeah, I guess so," she said, and smiled.

CHAPTER 29

WE WENT BACK OUT THE GATE INTO THE STREET. WE walked back down it and we went back in the gate to our tree and walked back down across the lawn to it. She sat back down with her back up against it and I lay back down sideways to her with my head in her lap, again. As I was doing it a flash of light caught my eye. I looked back down into the grass for it, but I didn't see it, again. But as I looked down into it I realized for the first time how many millions of leaves of grass were in the world. I wondered if it was even possible to count so many? I got frustrated as I looked down at it and I lay back down and put my head back in her lap. I looked up through the branches at the summer blue sky.

"I love the color of the sky."

"Yeah, I do, too."

"It's relaxing looking up at it?"

"Yeah, it is."

"This is a nice spot, here."

"Yeah, uh-huh."

"We lucked out, again, today, eh?"

"You mean, by finding it?"

"Yeah."

"Yeah, we sure did."

"I wish life was like this all the time?"

She smiled at me.

"It would be so great, eh?"

"Yeah, it sure would."

"We wouldn't have a care in the world?"

"No, we sure wouldn't?"

We watched a yacht going into the Lock. A second one was coming behind it. There were young couples on both. They both disappeared in behind the government-looking building. A third one, three times longer, was coming along behind them. Two old couples were sitting out on the captain's deck drinking cocktails and taking in the view. They waved to us and we waved back to them. Small dogs were sitting on the women laps. The men wore captain's uniforms.

Sometimes," I said, "I wonder if the rich people are as happy as they seem to be. They have enough money to buy everything that they want. They live in mansions with big fenced-in yards. They drive new cars and take long fancy vacations. But I still wonder sometimes if they're as happy as they seem to be. Or if it just seems that way to us because of all their money."

"Yeah, I wonder about that, sometimes, too."

"It takes a lot to work to keep all those things up. You have to wonder if it's even worth it to own so many?"

She didn't say anything.

"But I guess we can't know everything, eh? My dad seems to think that they're happy. He says that they have enough money to hire somebody to fix their things for them. And, being that he's a lot older than us, he's probably right about it, eh? But it's like I said about it, too: we can't know everything?"

She didn't say anything.

"It's funny how things get important to you when you're old, eh? It seems like all you do is sit around your house and worry about paying your bills. You never go out by yourself, anymore. Nothing that you do even looks interesting to most people. You sure don't lay down under a tree all day like we're doing, now. It's too bad that it has to be like that. But I guess that it has to be, or else it wouldn't. We'll probably get to be like that when we get old, too? We'll forget about the things that we did when we were young."

"I can't imagine my folks laying down here under this tree, all day."

"No, I can't imagine mine doing it, either. Who wants to get old, eh?"

"Yeah, that's for sure?"

"But, I guess there's nothing that we can do about it, eh?"

"No, I guess not."

I rolled down off her lap and I pulled her down to me. I kissed her and I hugged her and I got on top of her and moved on her like I was doing it. The guys at school called it dry-fucking. They did it to their girlfriends who wouldn't go all the way with them. The next day at school they complained about having blue balls. They said that it was extremely painful. What a name for it, I thought, blue balls? I wondered if their balls actually turned blue.

CHAPTER 30

"LOOK IT, A CHIPMUNK?"

"Oh, I see it?"

It leaped up to us and it sat up on its hind legs and chattered. It was brown except the white streak down its belly. I tried to coax it closer to us, but it got back down on its four feet and leaped away. It searched here and there in the grass for food. It climbed a tree by the big government-looking building and it sat up on a branch and chattered, again.

It went on up to what looked like its nest.

"Maybe it has babies in it?"

"Yeah, that could be?"

"When do they have them? Do you know?"

"No, I don't know. But I think it's in the spring."

"I'm hungry, again. What about you?"

"Yeah, I am, too."

"It must be suppertime, by now? Are you eating with us, today?"

"Yeah, I am, if you want me to?"

"Yeah, I do. I'm sorry that I didn't ask you, yesterday."

"That's okay."

"We better go, now? You know how my Mom is?"

"Yeah, okay."

"She's probably got supper started, by now?"

"Yeah, she probably does."

As she got up I saw a piece of grass sticking to her butt.

"Stop for a minute, Jackie. There's a piece of grass sticking to your pants."

She looked to see it.

"It's on the back of them."

She leaned back to see it.

As I brushed it off her eyes flashed.

"There, it's off, now. But now there's a grass stain there."

"I'll soak them in soap and water when I get home."

"They look like they're brand new."

"Yeah, they are. This is the first time that I've worn them."

We walked up across lawn and we went out through the gate. We started walk back down Portage to her house. The big shiny new SUVs and trucks were still in the street. It was Labor Day Weekend, the last hurrah of the tourist season. We turned off onto Barbeau and we walked over to her house and went inside.

Her Mom looked up at us.

"You got here just in time. We just sat down to eat."

"Mom, I'm sorry we're late."

Bunny ignored her.

Instead, she looked at me.

"Cortney, you're always welcome to stay and eat with us. We want you to feel at home here."

"Thank you."

We sat down at the table. Her Mom started the platter of pork and carrots and potatoes around it. Armand took what he wanted and passed it to us. We helped ourselves and we passed it back to her Mom. She set it back down on the table in front of her. Now she started the platter of apple sauce and pineapple around the table. It went around it like the platter before it. It came back to her and she set it back down on the table in front of her, too.

We all made BLTs for ourselves.

"BLTs are my favorite sandwich," I said, and smiled.

Bunny smiled down the table at me. Willis looked up at me and when I smiled at him he looked back down.

Armand was cutting his meat for him.

"Armand, when do you go back to work?"

He glanced up at me.

"I went back yesterday morning, uh-huh?"

"Oh? You work days, eh?"

"Yeah, I do. We only have the one shift down there."

"That's good. It's hard to beat days, eh?"

"Oh yeah, it is. I've worked nothing but days down there for ten years, now. Lately, I've been working ten-hour days. It makes for an awful long week."

"Yeah, it does. But the money is good, eh?"

"Yeah, it is. But even still I'm not so sure that it's worth it. Not with the wages being so low down there to begin with."

He sat back up.

"Oh really?"

"Yeah. At least that's how I see it. Somebody else might see it different. But as for me, if I didn't have to stay and do it, I wouldn't. But, as it is now, I don't have a say in the matter, and I have to stay."

"It's too bad that they're so low, eh?"

"Yeah, it is. But I don't think that they would be, if we had ourselves a union. But as it is now, we don't have ourselves one down there. So, I guess that they will always be low?"

"Yeah, they most likely always will?" I said.

We didn't talk much, after that. We washed down our sandwiches with our glasses of milk. Armand finished eating his first and he got back up and went out into the living room. I finished eating mine next and I got back up and went out into it with him. I sat down on the couch by him and we watched the evening news, together. Willis came in and he sat down and bounced in his chair. Jackie stayed behind in the kitchen with her mother. They washed the dishes and they came in and sat down with us, too. Shortly Bunny got back up and went off upstairs. Armand and Willis stayed and watched Big Valley with us. They got back up and they went off into their bedroom. Jackie and I watched Gun Smoke, together.

I fell asleep as I watched it.

I woke up to the late news.

"I must have gone to sleep, eh?"

"Yeah, you did. You slept through the whole show."

"What time is it?"

"It's after midnight, now."

"Wow, I guess I did go to sleep, eh?" I rubbed my eyes. "I feel like I closed my eyes and I opened them right back up. I'm tired for some reason, again, tonight?"

She took my hands into hers.

"It's no wonder that you're tired? Last night you slept in the city jail. Today, you spent the whole day outside. And now it's after midnight?"

"Things have a way of sneaking up on you, eh?"

"Yeah, they sure do."

"You looked tired, tonight, too."

"No, I'm okay."

I got up to go. "I really should get going. I can barely keep my eyes open. I need to get to bed and get some sleep."

She got up with me. "I'll walk you out to the door," she said.

We walked out to the door, together. Outside it, we kissed and hugged out in the silvery moonlight and we said goodnight.

She went back inside, and I started off for home.

Tonight, the patches of fog were back in the streets, again. I walked around them, and I kept my clothes dry. I worried that they would get damp and stick to me and pull at me when I was trying to sleep later. That they would keep me awake. That I would get up in the morning still feeling tired, again. Tonight, the water puddles were back in the streets, too. I walked around them, and I kept my shoes dry. The porch lights were reflecting in them and, like before, lighting up the neighborhoods a little. I walked over to Portage and I turned off onto it and I walked up it to the gate into our tree. I got there, and it was padlocked, now. The barbed wire on the top of it kept me from climbing over it.

Disappointed, I left to search elsewhere.

I walked further up Portage. I came to a big old Catholic Church. I walked around it and I checked the doors into it. They all were locked. I walked around it a second time and I looked in to the shrubbery for a place to crawl into and to lie down out of sight of the street and go off to sleep. But I didn't find one.

Disappointed, I left to search elsewhere, again.

I walked still further up Portage. I came to an office building. I walked around it and I looked in the shrubbery, again. But I didn't find a place to sleep in it, either.

Disappointed, I left to search still elsewhere.

I turned off onto Bingham. I walked up to a public library. As I walked around it I saw a place in the shrubbery to sleep. I crawled into and I lay down out of sight of the street and went off to sleep. But somewhere in the night I woke up to a flashlight beam darting about near me. I lie there too scared to move. I listened as two men talked between themselves. One knelt down and when he stood back up, he held a man by the arm. The other man got him by the other arm and they dragged him off between them, his legs dragging stiffly across the lawn, out to their police cruiser waiting in the street. They shoved him into the back and they got into the front and drove off. I waited until they went around the corner and I got back up, and got back out of there, too.

BOOK FOUR

The Old Train Depot

CHAPTER 31

AHEAD THE OLD BRICK BUILDING LOOKED SQUATTY IN under its overhanging roof. The single naked light bulb out front on the flag pole barely lighted it up. There were cedar trees growing around it. I walked up to them and I looked in for a place to lie down. I saw one and I crawled into it and went off to sleep. But there were pebbles under me and they poked me whenever I moved. I sat back up and I brushed them aside and lie back down. But I missed some and they still poked me. I didn't sit back up. Instead I squirmed about and I got as comfortable as I could and went back to sleep. In the morning I woke up still tired and I got up and crawled back out. I walked across to the platform down the side of the building and sat down on it. There were baggage carts on it. There were railroad tracks down along the side of it. The old brick building was an old abandoned railroad station. I waited for the sun to come up and I warmed up and stayed and waited for the day to warm up. It warmed up and I got back up and walked back across to the cedar trees. I broke off branches and I made a bed of them for myself and I lay down on it and went back to sleep.

I was doing this every day.

In the morning I was getting up and I was walking across to the loading platform and sitting down and warming up in sun. I was waiting for the day to warm up and I was getting back up and walking up to the corner gas station and cleaning up in the bathroom. I was walking back into town and Jackie and I were eating breakfast together and we were walking downtown and going window-shopping. We were walking over to our tree and we were snuggling up under it and kissing and hugging and taking little snoozes in the sun, and dry-fucking. Lunchtime, we were eating up at the Delmar and, at suppertime, we were walking back to her house and eating with her folks. They were going out into the living room and watching tv and we were following them out and watching it with them. Bedtime, Bunny was getting back up and going off upstairs; Armand and Willis were getting back up and going off into their bedroom; Jackie and I were snuggling up on the couch and watching movies late into the night. We were getting back up and we were walking out to the door, together. Outside it, were we kissing and hugging out in the cold dark and saying goodnight.

Wednesday night's I hitchhiked back home. I wanted to get a good night's sleep in my own bed. In the morning's I got up and I walked up to the lodge and reported for work. Tonight, the first car to come along belonged to my Uncle Carl. He stopped and he picked me up and took me back home. He dropped me off out front and I jumped the ditch and I walked through the yard and up to the door and in.

My Mom looked up at me.

"Well, my goodness, look whose back home. This certainly is a pleasant surprise. What, may I ask, brings you back this soon?"

I didn't say anything.

"It's good to see you back home again, alive and all in one piece. I was beginning to worry about you. I didn't know where I would begin to look for you, if I needed to. Well, my dear, where have you been keeping yourself. What have you been doing?"

"I've been in town."

"Oh, so you've been in town? I had no idea where to look?"

I didn't say anything.

"I've missed seeing you around here. I'm happy to see you back home, again."

"Well, I'm okay?"

"Yes, you are okay? But you've been gone an awful long time?"

"Well, I can take care of myself."

"Oh, I'm sorry. I didn't mean to pry."

I said nothing.

"What brings you back, tonight? I mean why tonight? Why not tomorrow night, or even the night after that?"

I didn't say anything.

"What makes one night any different from another?"

"I start work in the morning."

"Oh, you start work in the morning? You found a job for yourself? Well, how about that? Where will you work? What will you do there?"

"I'll be waiting tables up at the resort."

"Oh, you'll be waiting tables up at the resort? Well, that certainly is good news? I had no idea that you were even out looking for a job."

I said nothing.

She didn't either, now. She was caught by surprise with the news. Her stride was broken. She wasn't sure what to say to me, now. She sat back in her chair as if to think about it.

"Yeah, I'll be waiting tables, up there," I said, feeling in control myself, now. "And I'll be helping out with maintenance work."

"Well, that is such good news. What a wonderful surprise: You went out and you found a job for yourself." She put her hand on her chin. "But what about your interest in town? Won't having a job, interfere with that?"

"I have to get up early."

"Congratulations on the job?"

"Thank you," I said.

I started up the stairs.

"Well, maybe now we'll see more of you around here?"

I ignored her, again.

I went upstairs into my bedroom and I got undressed and pulled the blankets back on my bed and got into it. I cuddle down under them and I went off to sleep. I woke up in the morning to the smell of bacon and eggs cooking downstairs in the kitchen. I got up and I went down and sat down at the table with my Mom. We ate breakfast, together. I got back up and I showered and shaved, and I went out the door and walked out through the yard and jumped the ditch and got out onto the blacktop. I started to walk up to the resort. They were training me to be a waiter. I would be meeting new people. I turned off into the driveway and I looked up at the gravel roadbed ahead. There was steam rising up out of it. The sun was already taking over the day. It was going to be another scorcher. I walked in to the parking lot and I looked up at the ski runs and thought of how, in the summer, they looked like hiking trails. I looked over at the lodge and I thought of how its big windows reflected the sunlight like mirrors. I saw guests eating their break-fast out on the back veranda. I saw other guests riding the chairlift up to the top of the mountain. Still others were up on horses riding them off onto trails into the woods. It was a busy place for so early in the morning. I walked over to the lodge and I climbed up the stairs to the door and I opened it and went in and walked across the lobby and asked the receptionist for directions into the kitchen. She said to walk through the dining room. I walked through it looking up out its windows at the ski slopes. She said to go through the swing-ing doors at the far end of it. I went through them and I bumped into Mr. Swartz. I apologized to him and he assured me that it was okay. We shook hands and we introduced ourselves. He reached down into the box at his side and he bought up a white dinner jacket and a black bowtie, and gave them both to me. He introduced me to the other waiters and then went back to his talk. He said that we weren't going to get all the minimum wage. That our tips would be considered as part of our wages. He talked about getting along with the kitchen staff and we looked over the dining room menu, together. He helped us with the few French words on it. We took serving trays out into the dining room and we practiced serving tables with them. We walked over to the bar, together. He talked about getting along with the bar staff and we looked over the menu, together. He helped us with the few French words on it, too. We took cocktail trays out into the bar lounge and we practiced serving drinks with them. We walked back to the dining room, together. We set the tables and we straightened out the chairs around them and we got everything ready for our first guests.

The receptionist brought the guests into the dining room. She sat them down at the tables and she walked over and gave them to us in turns. We would soon learn that all we could handle and still do a good job were three or four tables a piece. The worst accident of the evening was a dropped coffee pot that shattered on the table and spilled hot coffee all across it. Luckily for our guests they jumped and they scattered in time and nobody got hurt. Other than for that the evening went by uneventfully. I kept my head about myself and I worked hard and didn't drop anything. I earned sixty dollars in tips. I got so excited about it that I counted it over three times. I hurried out the door and I ran out to the blacktop and I started down it with my hands held out front of me in case I bumped into a bear. I ran up to the house and into it and I went upstairs to bed and off to sleep.

I got up in the morning and I walked over to the bar and called Jackie. She answered the phone on the first ring. I told her that I loved her, and she said that she loved me, too. I told her about my first day at work and she told me about her and Ellie walking downtown later, and laying away school clothes. It was good to hear her voice, again. Our phone calls were the high point of my days. I called her again before I left for work and we made plans to see each other later and, after we hung up, I missed her even more. I could barely wait to go and see her and touch her. I walked up to the lodge and I waited tables in the dining room and, after work, I ran back home and I hurried up the stairs to bed and went off to sleep. I wanted to get as much rest as I could before I got back up in the morning and I hitchhiked back in to town and saw Jackie.

CHAPTER 32

I LOOKED OUT THE RAIN-SPLATTERED WINDOW. THE large drops came straight down. They splattered the length of the beach road. I couldn't see down through them to the lake. I didn't want to go out into it, but I knew if I wanted to see Jackie I would have to. I went out the door and I hurried out through the yard and jumped the ditch. I got out onto the blacktop and I started to walk down it. I was down past the fishery when a car stopped and picked me up. It took me in to the Soo and it dropped me off downtown.

I walked out to her place.

I knocked on the door and she opened it. She was surprised to see me so wet.

"My God, Cortney, you're soaking wet."

"Yeah, I am. You got a towel, handy?"

"Wait here. I'll get you one."

She hurried off to the bathroom.

The rain ran down off my forehead into my eyes. I wiped it away with both hands. I could barely see.

Willis ran in from the living room.

"Hi, Cortney."

"Hi, Willis. How are you, today?"

"Is Jackie your girlfriend, Cortney?"

"Yes, Willis, she is."

Jackie handed the towel to me.

"Thank you," I said, and wiped my face. "I can't remember it raining this hard. I haven't been this wet in a long time."

"Cortney, did you get wet?"

"Yeah, Willis, I sure did. It's raining hard out?"

He ran back into the living room.

"Would you like a cup of coffee? It'll warm you up?"

"Yeah, thanks. I would."

"It's fresh. Dad made it before he went to work."

I told her what I liked in it.

"Here's your towel back. Thanks for getting it for me."

"You're very welcome," she said.

She set it aside, and handed the coffee to me.

"Thank you. How are you, today?"

"I'm okay."

"I missed you."

"I missed you, too."

We kissed and hugged.

"I have something to tell you?"

"Oh, you do?" she said.

"Yeah, I do," I said. "Take a wild guess at what you think it is."

"Oh, I don't know. What?"

"Take a wild guess, first. It's something that we talked about?"

"Actually, I don't have any idea."

"Well, try guessing, once, first, okay?"

"Well, okay, let's see? You found a car to buy?"

"Wow, you're right. You got it on the first try. Yeah, I found a car to buy."

"Wow, you really did?"

"Yeah, I really did."

"Wow, that's so great."

"Yeah, it's a nice one, too. It's a '05 Ford Mustang. It has a big V-8 in it with lots of horsepower. A guy up at work has it for sale. He said that I could buy it for twenty-seven hundred dollars. I asked him if he'd hold it for me until I got the money for it, and he said that he would."

"Is that a good price for it?"

"Heck, yeah, that's a really good price for it. Wait until you see it, you'll love it."

"If you love it, already, it must be nice?"

"Yeah, it is. I love everything about it. You open the doors and these red lights come on under the dash. It has Bose Sound in it, Hollywood mufflers, a wind deflector over the windshield, tinted windows, everything."

"Wow, it sounds nice."

"Yeah, it is, too. What's more, it'll soon be mine. Now we can go wherever we want to. We won't have walk anywhere, ever again."

"You won't have into hitchhike into town and see me. Or get stuck in here overnight and have to sleep in the city jail."

"Yeah, and now we can drive out to the movies, sometimes, too."

"Yeah, we can? I'm surprised you found one so soon."

"Yeah, I am too."

We kissed and hugged, again.

"You can pick me up at school, sometimes, now, too?"

"Yeah, I can?" I hadn't thought of it. But it was like her. She always thought about us first no matter what else was going on.

She was still in her pajamas.

"I'm going upstairs to change. I'm taking off this funny hat, too."

We both smiled a little.

Willis ran back in from the living room.

"Willis, you're back. It's good to see you, again."

He leaned back on the refrigerator. He began to bang his head on it.

"Willis, you shouldn't do that. You'll get a big bump on your head."

He ignored me.

"Go ahead, Willis, bang your head on it."

He banged his head on it.

"Willis, where's your Dad at? Do you know?"

He ignored me, again.

That was a dumb question, I thought. It's Monday morning and he's at work. But where's his Mom? I don't see her around here, anywhere?

"Where's your mother at, Willis?"

He ignored me, again. The heck with him, I thought. If he won't talk to me, I won't talk to him, either. I didn't say another word to him. Or even look at him, again. I waited quietly for Jackie.

She came back in wearing a blouse.

"You look good in your blouse."

"Thank you."

"It fits you perfectly."

"Thank you."

We both smiled a little.

"Do you want to go for a walk?"

"Yeah, I do. But Mom went out to an auction with a friend of hers. She left Willis here for me to watch. It looks like we're stuck here with him, today?"

"Oh, really?"

"Yeah, really?"

"Well, I guess there's nothing we can do about it?"

"No, I guess not." She thought about it. "But if we really wanted to go somewhere, we could take him with us?"

I thought about it, too.

"Yeah, but if we really wanted to go somewhere, we could take him with us. Or, we could stay here with him. Or we could leave him here alone and go off by ourselves, somewhere. Or we could even…"

"Cortney, what are you doing?"

"Oh nothing. I'm trying to be funny."

"Cortney, I love you."

"I love you, too, Jackie."

We kissed and hugged, again.

We walked out into the living room. We sat down on the couch. She picked up a magazine and held it up by her face.

"You'll never guess what Willis did, today?"

"No, probably not? What did he do?"

"He killed the little kitten that our Uncle Mike brought over for us. He broke the poor little thing's neck. Dad thinks that he didn't do it on purpose. That it was an accident of some kind. But

he kept playing with it even after it was dead. Dad asked him if he
knew that it was dead, and he said he didn't. But Dad thinks that
he did. Its body was stiff, already."

"Wow, that's bizarre."

"Yeah, it is. Now Dad thinks that there's something wrong
with him, too? He tried to talk to him about it later. But all he
would say to him is that he didn't do it."

"Wow, that's so bizarre, eh?"

"Yeah, it is. But anyhow, he got a good spanking for it."

"He needs some help, eh?"

"Yeah, he does. He definitely has something wrong with him?"

She sat the magazine back down.

We turned on the tv and we watched Mike and Molly. We
went out into the kitchen and we sat down at the table and played
a couple hands of Michigan Rummy. Willis got hungry and she got
back up and made a peanut butter and jelly sandwich for him. He
ate it and we went back out into the living room. We sat back down
on the couch and watched The Office, together.

We both grew tired of it.

"Would you like to go for a walk?"

"Sure, where to?"

"Wherever you'd like to go?"

"We can walk down to the corner store, and get an ice cream
cone, if you want to?"

"Yean, I do. That sounds fun."

"Willis, we're walking down to the corner store, and getting
an ice cream cone. Do you want to come with us?"

He ignored her.

"He'll come," she said. "I'll make him come, if I have to."

Willis came without a problem. We held hands and he walked
between us. When we got down near the store he ran off ahead of
us. He went up to a couple little boys playing out on the sidewalk
in front of it. They were pushing their little cars around on it. He
took one away from them and when they tried to get it back from
them he pushed them both down. It happened so fast that Jackie

and I could barely believe our eyes. I ran up and I took the little car back away from him and I gave it back to the little boys. I helped them both get back up onto their feet. I took Willis by the hand and I hustled him back up the sidewalk. I looked back at them and they both were standing back there and watching us go, and crying. I worried that their parents would come out and that there would be hell to pay. Jackie scolded Willis really good for it on the way back to the house. We went into it and he went off alone into his bedroom. Jackie and I sat back down on the couch, together. Suddenly the living room lighted up. There was a loud thunderclap above the house. All the windows in it rattled. It down poured and made a racket on the roof. Willis ran back out of the bedroom and over to Jackie where he sat down by her and cuddled in really close.

CHAPTER 33

BUNNY GOT HOME AT FIVE-THIRTY. SHE STARTED SUPPER
for us. Armand got home at six still dirty from his work. He took
his shower and his face shone. Bunny put the food on the table and
we sat down and ate it. Armand got back up, and went out into the
living room. I got back up, and followed him out into it. We both
sat down on the couch and watched the evening news, together.
Willis came in and bounced in his chair. Jackie stayed behind in the
kitchen with her mother. They washed the dishes and they came in
and sat down with us, too.

We all watched the evening news.

"Would you like to go for a walk?" I said.

"Sure, where to?"

"Wherever you'd like to?"

She smiled a little.

As I got up I looked out the window. The raindrops on the
flowers were big. They were big on the porch railings, too. I never
saw them so big. The leaves and the grass were the wettest and
the prettiest color of green that I ever saw. I never saw them so
pretty, before?

They all were glistening in sunlight.

"Wow, it's pretty out there," I said. "There are big drops of
rain on everything in the yard. I never saw them so big or so pretty.
The whole yard is glistening with them."

Armand got up, and looked for himself.

"Yeah, it sure is."

Jackie got up, and looked for herself, too.

"Wow, is it ever pretty out there. I never saw it so pretty,
before, either."

We held hands and we went out the door, together. We stood
on the porch and we looked around at the yard. It looked like you
always wanted it to look. We walked out the driveway looking to

either side at it. We stood in the middle of the street and we looked back at it. We couldn't get enough of it. We looked in to the neighbor's yard. There were big drops of rain glistening on everything in it, too. We couldn't get enough of it, either.

"Let's walk down to the river, and see what it looks like?" I said.

She both nodded, and smiled.

We stood on the dock and we looked out at the river. A mist hung over it. The whitecaps curled down over onto and splashed in the sunlight. Ships moved through it, buildings surrounded it, houses up on the slopes above it loomed over it; they all glistened in the sunlight, too. It was prettier than all hell. I never saw it so goddamn pretty. We couldn't get enough of it, either. It was Mother Nature at her best: showing us how beautiful she could be. How she could make things glisten in the sunlight. But we all knew her for her nastiness, too. How she made the earthquakes, the tornados and the hurricanes that killed people. I looked up at the homes on the slopes above Soo, Ontario. I thought about the homes up on the slopes above Sarajevo, Bosnia. The people froze to death in them when their heat got shut off by the war. I wondered what would happen to the people of Soo, Ontario, if their heat got shut off by a war? Would they freeze to death in their houses, too? I wondered about Jackie and me and what would have become us if I told her when we were out on the island, together, what my true feelings were about nature. That it was both beautiful, and ugly.

Would she still love me?

"Are you ready to go?"

"Yeah, if you are, I am?"

"Yeah, I am," I said.

We took a last look out at the river.

"The lower river is getting foggy," I said.

She looked down into it, too. But she didn't say anything about it. We held hands and we walked back out to the street. We walked back down it and turned off onto Barbeau. It was foggy, now. We walked around patches of it and we kept our clothes dry.

I didn't want mine to get damp and stick to me. They would pull at me when I was trying to sleep, later. I would lay awake all night and I would get up in the morning still feeling tired, again. We walked over to her house and we went into it and sat down on the couch. I noticed it was too quiet. I stood back up and I looked in to Armand's bedroom. Both he and Willis were asleep in it. I wondered where Bunny was.

"Where's your mother at, Jackie?"

"She's probably upstairs sleeping. They don't sleep together, anymore."

I didn't say anything.

"Or, she could be out at the bar?"

We turned on the tv and we watched a sitcom, together. I fell asleep watching it and when I woke back up my head was lying on her shoulder.

"I guess I fell asleep, eh?"

"Yeah, you did. You missed most of the show."

"I'm feeling tired again tonight for some reason. I should probably go home, and go to bed."

"I wish you could stay here."

"Oh, you do? Really?"

"Yeah, I do. I worry about you sleeping out on the ground. That you'll catch a bad cold, or something."

"Yeah, I do, too."

She didn't say anything.

I stood up to go.

"I should probably go, eh?"

She got up, now, too.

"I'll walk out to the door with you," she said.

We held hands and we walked out to the door. Outside it, we kissed and hugged out in the misty moonlight and we said goodnight. She went back inside, and I started off for the depot. The fog was still in the streets. Patches of it were wrapped around the streetlights. The night was spooky. I put my hands into my pockets and I doubled them up into fists and got myself ready to punch somebody and run off, if I had to. I got out to the depot and I crawled into my bed of cedar boughs. I lay down on them and I went off to sleep. But whenever I moved my clothes stuck to me. They pulled at me and they woke me back up. I got back up and I walked across to the loading platform and lay down on it. But the boards were hard and I couldn't get comfortable. I went to sleep but by morning I was back awake a dozen time. I got up still tired again. I walked up to the corner gas station and I cleaned up in the bathroom and walked back in and saw Jackie.

We ate breakfast together and we walked downtown to our tree. We lay down under it and we snuggled on the grass and spent the rest of the morning there. Lunchtime, we got back up and we walked up to the Delmar. We walked through to back of it and we sat down in a booth and ordered hamburgers and cokes. They came and we both ate, and talked. Supper time, we walked back down Portage and over on Barbeau to her house. We ate it with her folks and they got back up and went out into the living room and we got back up and followed them out into it and watched a movie with them. They got back up and they went off to their bedrooms and we snuggled up on the couch and watched another movie. Outside the door later, we kissed and hugged out in the light of the silvery moon and we said goodnight. She went back inside and I walked out to the highway and stuck out my thumb. The first car to come along belonged to my neighbor. He picked me up and he took me back home. He dropped me off out front and I walked through the yard and up to the house and into it and I climbed up the stairs into my bedroom and I got into bed and went off to sleep.

In the morning I called Jackie.

"Hello."

"Hi, Jackie."

"Hi. Did you make it home, alright?"

"Yeah, I did."

"Good. I worried about you?"

"Oh?"

"Yeah, I always do. I worry that no one will stop for you. Or that a bear will get you, or something."

"Well, I'm okay."

"That's good."

"How are you, today?"

"I'm okay. But I can't say as much for Willis."

"Oh, what happened to him?"

"Well, I'm not sure what did? But when Mom got up this morning she found him slumped down in his chair. She thought that he was sleeping. But she noticed that his breathing was shallow. She shook him but she couldn't wake him up. She called Dad at work and he said to take him down to the doctor. That's where they are, now."

"Wow, that's scary."

"Yeah, it is. Nothing like this has happened to him before. He's always been quite normal, at least physically."

"Yeah, uh-huh?"

"Yeah. Maybe now they'll find out what's wrong with him?"

"Yeah, let's hope so, eh?"

"How are you, today?"

"I'm okay. It felt good to sleep in my bed, again."

"Yeah, I bet, especially after sleeping out on the ground."

"Yeah, that's for sure. I got some real sleep for a change, too."

"That's good. You needed it."

"Yeah, I did. Well, I better go. I have to get ready for work."

"Yeah, okay."

"Bye, Jackie, I love you."

"Bye, I love you too, Cortney."

We both hung up.

BOOK FIVE

I Get a Car

CHAPTER 34

BY MONDAY MORNING I WAS ANXIOUS TO SEE JACKIE again. I got out of bed and I ate breakfast with my Mom. I walked out to the blacktop and I started to walk down it. I got down past the fishery before a car stopped and picked me up. It took me into the Soo and it dropped me off downtown. I walked out to her place and as I knocked on the door she opened it.

"Hi."

"Hi, Jackie."

We kissed and hugged.

She felt new to me, again.

"I missed you."

"I missed you, too."

I sensed something was wrong.

"How are things, really?"

"Actually, they're not good."

"Oh?"

"Yeah, actually they're not good, at all."

"Oh, what's wrong?"

"It's my mother. She didn't come home last night. She got into a fight at the bar and now she's in jail. She called here but Dad won't go down and get her out." Her voice cracked. "He said she could stay in there."

"She must be furious?"

"Yeah, she is. But not as much as Dad. She called here again but he left for work."

I felt like hugging her, but I didn't.

"Where's Willis at?"

"He's in the living room."

"How is he doing?"

"He's doing okay?"

"What did his doctor say about him?"

"He said that he couldn't find anything wrong with him."

"Did he know why he passed out?"

"No. But he thinks that it could have been an anxiety attack. Other than that, he didn't seem to know."

"That's strange, eh? You'd think he'd know more?"

"Yeah, you would. But he did prescribe some nerve pills for him. He said that he's underweight and that he should be taking vitamin pills, too. But that's all he'd say."

"Well, at least, it was something?"

"Yeah, I guess so, eh?"

"I missed you, Jackie."

"I missed you too, Cortney."

We kissed and hugged, again.

"Is there anything that you'd like to do, today? Or that you need to do, or whatever?"

"Yeah, actually there is. But I should stay here in case Mom calls, again. But that could pointless. Because they might not let her. And even if they do, there's nothing that I can do anyway. Dad will have to go down and get her out."

"Well, we can stay here if you think we should. There's nothing that I need to do, today. I would like to go off by ourselves, again. But that can wait until, later."

"Yeah, uh-huh?"

"Yeah, I've been feeling cooped up, again."

"Well, if it's okay with you, Willis can come with us? We don't have to stay here with him."

"What does he like to do?"

"Actually, I don't care what he likes to do. We can spend the whole day outside, too, if you want to."

I didn't say anything.

"We can leave, now, too, if you want to."

"Well, let's go for a walk, then?"

"Dad will go down from work and get Mom out."

I looked in to the living room. Willis was sitting in his chair. He wasn't bouncing in it. He was looking at the wall ahead. I looked in to see what was on it. There was nothing on it. I walked in and I picked him up. He squirmed in my arms and I put him back down. Jackie came in and she took his hand and pulled him off his chair. I took his other hand and the three of us walked out to the door, together. Outside it, we struck off for downtown. When Willis was content to walk between us and he didn't run off ahead we both wondered why. We decided that it was the effects of his medication. We walked down to Frank's Place and we went inside and drank a cup of coffee. We walked over to our tree and we lay down under it and snuggled up on the grass. Shortly Willis got back up. He walked up to the fence and he held onto it above his head and swung back and forth. I fell asleep as I watch him do it. When I woke back up he was lying by Jackie.

He said that he was hungry.

"Jackie, I have enough money on me, today, if you want to eat uptown."

"Actually, I'm not hungry?"

"Actually, I'm not, either. I guess only Willis is, eh?"

"Yeah, I guess so."

"Well, I could walk up to the store, and get something for him, and bring it back here?"

"Actually, I'm a little hungry. But don't feel like going, anywhere."

"That's funny. Because I'm actually a little hungry, too. But I don't feel like going anywhere, either. Strange, eh?"

She didn't say anything.

"Well okay, I'll walk up to the store, and get something for him, and something for us, and bring it back here?"

"Yeah, okay?"

"What should I get for us?"

"Anything is okay by me?"

"You're an easy one to please, today."

"Yeah, I am. I'm just happy being here with you."

"Sweetheart, I love you."

"I love you, too, Cortney."

We kissed and hugged, again.

I walked up across the lawn and I went out the gate. I walked over to Ashmun and I walked up to Super Value. I went into it and I got a cart and pushed it through the aisles. I put a bag of potato chips and a package of Danish rolls into it. Over at the coolers I put in three small cartons of milk. I pushed it up to the cashier and I paid for them. I went back out into the street and I walked back down it imagining Jackie and Willis waiting for me under the tree and, for the briefest moment, I felt like we were a real family. I went back into the gate and I walked down across the lawn and sat back down with them. I passed out the cartons of milk and the Danish rolls and potato chips. It turned out that Willis wasn't as hungry as he thought. But that both Jackie and I were hungrier than we thought. We ate ours and we ate what he left of his. Suppertime, we went back out the gate and we walked back down Portage to Barbeau and over on it to her house. She cooked a pizza and as she was taking it back out of the oven Bunny barged through the door. She slammed it shut behind her and she hurried through the kitchen and out into the living room and through it and back out the front door. Armand came in and he looked around for her and when he didn't see her he went off into the bathroom. We heard the water run and stop and he came back out and sat down at the table with us. He ate a slice of the pizza and he got back up and went back into it. Willis got up and followed him. We heard the water run and stop again and the two of them in the bathtub taking a bath, together.

We stayed at the table, and talked.

"I got paid again, today. I made five hundred dollars this week. Tomorrow I'm getting up early and I'm walking up to the resort and talking to Chet about buying his car."

She didn't say anything.

"I going to talk to the manager about it, too. I'm going to ask him if he will give me an advance on my pay. If he gives it to me, I'll pay Chet for his car and I'll drive it to town and show it to you.

And, if you want to, we can drive out to the A&W, and get something to eat."

She still didn't say anything.

"You're quiet, today?"

"I'm okay," she said, and smiled.

"Well, anyhow, we'll eat, and we'll drive out to the movies."

"Wow," she said, "we'll actually have our own car. Now we can go wherever we want to. We won't have walk anywhere, ever again."

"Things are really changing for us, eh?"

"Yeah, they sure are?" she said.

We both smiled.

CHAPTER 35

I WENT OUT INTO THE LIVING ROOM AND I SAT DOWN ON the couch. I watched the evening news. Jackie stayed behind in the kitchen. She picked up the dishes and she came in and sat down with me. Armand and Willis walked through on the way to their bedroom. Shortly they came back out wearing their pajamas. They sat down, and they watched the news with us. Shortly they got back up and they went back into their bedroom. We stayed and watched a movie and we got back up and walked out to the door, together. Outside it, we kissed and hugged out in the cold dark and said goodnight.

"I love you."

"I love you, too."

"See you later, okay?"

"Yeah, okay, see you," she said.

She went back inside, and I struck off for the depot.

I crawled into my bed of cedar boughs and I squirmed about on it. I got as comfortable as I could and went off to sleep. But somewhere in the night it got cold and I woke back up. I lay there and I waited for the sun to come up. I got up and I walked across to the loading platform and I sat down on it and warmed up. I waited for the day to warm up and I got back up and walked up to the corner gas station. I cleaned up in the bathroom and I walked back in to Jackie's. I knocked on the door and when she opened it she was still wearing her pajamas. She still looked tired and I told her to go back to bed and to get some more sleep. That I would come back later. We kissed and hugged and we said goodbye. She went back in and I struck off for Frank's Place. I went into it and I sat down in a booth and ordered a cup of coffee. My waitress brought it out to me and I took my time and drank it. I got back up and I paid for it on the way back out. I walked back down Portage to her house and when I went into it her mother was back home. We would be free to go off by ourselves, again. We ate breakfast together and we hurried out the door. We walk up town and we went window shopping and walked over to our tree. We lay down in the green grass and we snuggled up and took little snoozes in the sun. We looked up at the homes on the slopes above Soo, Ontario. We wondered what it was like to live in them. Suppertime, we walked back to her house and she put a pizza into the oven. She cooked it and she took it back out and put it onto the table. We sat down and we ate it and got back up. We walked out into the living room and we snuggled up on the couch and watched movies late into the night. We walked out to the door, together. Outside it, we kissed and hugged out in the silvery moonlight and we said goodnight.

She went back inside, and I struck off for home.

I needed to get a good night's sleep in my bed. Tomorrow I was walking up to the lodge and talking to Mr. Schwartz about the advance on my pay. I walked out to the highway and I stuck out my thumb. The first car to come along stopped for me and picked me up. I was back home and upstairs in bed by two o'clock. In the morning I got up and I went downstairs. When my Mom saw that I was back home she wondered what it meant. I told her about getting the advance on my pay and buying Chet's car with it. She thought that it was a good idea. She cooked breakfast for us and she put it on the table. We sat down and ate it. As she was picking up the dishes I went out the door and walked out through the yard. I jumped the ditch and I got out onto the blacktop and walked up to the lodge. I went in to see Mr. Schwartz' and I asked him for the advance on my pay. He gave it to me and I paid Chet for his car. I walked out into the parking lot and I got into it. I drove it into town and I showed it to Jackie. She got all excited about it. She smiled at me and she said how much she liked it. She couldn't say enough about it. We got into it and we drove out to the Dairy Queen. We bought ice cream cones. As we rode around town feeling as if we had arrived we ate them. Arrived where, we didn't know? That we were living on a higher plane, now. On what higher plane, we didn't know, either? We pulled into Rotary Park and we parked and watched the ships go by. We finished eating our ice creams and we drove down along the river. We pulled into Jack's Country Store. We went into it and we bought bags of potato chips and cans of pop. As we drove farther down along the river we snacked on them. We pulled into Sugar Loaf Mountain. We parked and we got out and climbed up to the top. We looked up and down the river for a ship. We didn't see one and we looked out across it at the mountains in Canada. They looked big out in the bright sun. We climbed back down and we got back into our car and drove further down along the river. We took the Neebish Island ferry across to the island. We rode around the outside of it looking out into the fields at the herds of buffalo. We took it back across it and we drove back up along it, looking out through the trees at it, again. Back up in the Soo we pulled into Clyde's and ordered hotdogs and cokes. They came, and we pulled up by the river to eat. We left, and we drove out to the drive-in movies. We paid at the gate and we drove through to the back. We parked, and we snuggled and kissed and hugged. We left before the movie started and we drove off into the country. We pulled into a gravel pit and we parked around back of a pile of it. We snuggled up and we kissed and hugged, again. Shortly we got back to where we left off at the movies. We stopped and, listening to Elvis Presley singing, 'Love Me Tender', we looked up at the night sky.

"Lots of stars out, tonight, eh?"

"Yeah, that's for sure."

"They come right down at you?"

"Yeah, they do."

"It's a black sky, bright star night."

"Yeah, it sure is."

I kissed her and hugged her and I helped her lie back down onto the seat and I got in between her legs and I put my hands up in under her blouse and fondled her breasts and I pushed myself up and I reached up under her skirt and pulled her panties down and off her legs and I undid my belt buckle and I unsnapped my jeans and pushed them both down and off my legs and I lay back down in between hers and did it to her: now all I remember is it feeling tight and breathing hard and her hands moving in my hair and her saying, "I love you, I love you, I love you," over and over again: the little whimpers and cries and pushing myself up with my arms and holding myself above her and looking down at where I knew she was lying in the dark beneath me but seeing only the reflection of the starlight in her eyes.

"Jackie, are you okay?"

She didn't say anything.

I lay back down on her and I squirted in her and got off.

"I'm sorry for doing it to you, again," I said.

She said nothing.

I kissed and hugged her to try and make up for it. We pulled our clothes back on and we drove back in to town. We parked out front of her house and we went into it and lay down on the couch. We snuggled up on it and we watched the movies far into the night, again. We got back up and we walked out to the door, together. Outside it, we kissed and hugged out in the cold dark and we said goodnight.

I called her in the morning.

"Hello."

"Hi, Jackie."

"Hi, Cortney."

"How are you, today?"

"I'm okay. Did you make it home, alright?"

"Yeah, I did. The car ran good."

"Cortney, I love you."

"I love you too, Jackie."

"Even after last night, you do?"

"Yeah, even more."

"Good, I hope so. I love you more, too."

"Good."

"Things are really quiet in here, today."

"Oh, yeah?"

"Yeah, they're pretty much back to normal."

"That's good to hear..."

"...if there is a normal around here?"

I didn't say anything.

"I wish I could see you before Monday."

"Oh yeah...?"

"Yeah, but you get off work so late, eh?"

"Yeah, I do."

"School starts in two weeks?"

"Yeah it does?"

"Our lives are really going to change, then."

"Yeah, I know."

"Cortney, I love you."

"I love you too, Jackie."

"Honey, come in and see me, tonight, okay?"

"Yeah okay, Honey, I will. I won't be there until eleven though."

"That's okay."

"Okay, Sweetheart. I'll see you, then."

"Okay, I love you."

"I love you, too," I said.

I drove in to town and I saw her. She was sitting out on the front steps waiting for me. She walked out to the car and she got into it with me. We drove down to Clyde's and we ordered hamburgers and cokes. They came, and we pulled up by the river to eat.

I apologized to her, again, as we ate.

CHAPTER 36

MR. SWARTZ WANTED TO SEE ME IN HIS OFFICE. CHET delivered the message to me. I was in the kitchen making up bread-baskets at the time.

"Right now," I said.

"Yeah, he said for you to come right in."

I stopped making them up. I couldn't think of anything I did wrong. I kept my cool and I went to see him. I walked out through the dining room and I went across the lobby and up to his secretary's desk.

She smiled up at me.

"Mr. Swartz wants to see me."

"Please go right in, Cortney."

"Thank you," I said, and walked by her.

I opened the door and Mr. Swartz got up from behind his desk.

"Please come in, Cortney."

He walked around it with his hand out. I took it and we both shook, and smiled.

"Thanks, Cortney, for coming in to see me. Before we get started, I want you to know how much I appreciate your work. I've heard nothing but good remarks about it. This morning I've asked you in to talk to you about working overtime for us. We're getting the slopes ready for the winter season. There's still lots of work to do. And, in light of those good remarks, I've decided to offer it to you, first. Well, how do you feel about it, Cortney? Is it something that interests you?"

I didn't realize that I was doing that good of a job. But I was happy to hear him say it. I was happy too that he was offering it to me, first.

"When would I start, Mr. Swartz?"

"This Saturday, Cortney."

"Good, I'll take it. I can use the money. Thanks for offering it to me, first, too."

"Then, you are interested, Cortney?"

"Yes, I am, Mr. Swartz, very much so."

"Good. I thought that you would be."

He got back up from behind his desk and he walked around it with his hand out, again. I took it and we both shook, and smiled, like before.

"Mr. Beck will be your supervisor, Cortney. Please report to him in the morning when you first get here. He will be more than happy to help you with anything."

"Thank you, Mr. Swartz."

"Thank you, Cortney, for coming in to see me."

"You're welcome, Mr. Swartz. Thanks for thinking of me."

"Keep up the good work, Cortney," he said, and smiled.

I let myself back out the door. Jackie was on my mind as we talked. I hurried downstairs into the cafeteria and I called her. She answered the phone on the first ring.

"Hello."

"Hi, Jackie..."

"Oh, hi."

"I have something to tell you."

"Oh, you do?"

"Yeah, it's about my work."

"Oh, uh-huh?"

"Yeah, the manager asked me into his office. He asked me if I wanted to work overtime."

"Oh, what did you tell him?"

"I told him I did."

"Oh, you did?"

"Yeah, I did? But don't worry about it, Jackie? We'll still have time to see each other. I'll still come in after work and see you. But yeah, we won't see as much of each other. But the thing is, school is starting soon and we wouldn't have, anyway."

She didn't say anything.

"Are you still there?"

"Yeah, I am. I was thinking about what you said. Yeah, you're right; school is starting soon. I wish that it wasn't, but it is. But I also wish that we could still have seen as much of each other, until it does."

"Well, if it waited, we could have. But as it is, it didn't wait. But I think in the long run that it will be a good thing for us."

"Yeah, you're probably right. But I wish that it waited, too. But it's like you said, it didn't wait."

We both got quiet.

"Well, anyhow, it's been a great summer?"

"Yeah, it has."

"But it's sad that it's ending, like this?"

"Yeah, it is."

"Maybe I should have said, no?"

"No, you did the right thing. You do need the money."

"Yeah, I suppose I do, eh?"

"Yeah, you do. Don't worry about us, okay? Things will work out."

"Yeah, you're right. They most likely will."

"When will I see you, again?"

"I'll come in after work, tomorrow. We'll go out for a ride, somewhere."

"Sure, okay. I'll see you when you get here?"

"We can drive out to the A&W, and get something to eat, if you want to?"

"Yeah, I do. I love their food."

"Good. I love you, Sweetheart."

"I love you, too."

We both hung up.

The dining room was busy in the evening. I made twelve dollars in tips. We closed and I drove home and went to bed. In the morning I got up and I ate breakfast with my mom. As I went out the door she picked up the dishes. I got into the car and I drove up to the lodge and reported for work.

Mr. Beck went over my list of duties with me.

1. Sweep out the cafeteria, empty the wastebaskets
2. Haul the kitchen garbage to the burial pit
3. Clean the swimming pool, check the chlorine.
4. Work up on the slopes, cutting brush, etc.
5. Prepare for the Native Show.
6. All other duties as assigned...

He handed it to me, to look over for myself.

"Other than what's on that list," he said, "there are a few other odd jobs. But that list is pretty much it."

"Thank you, Mr. Beck. It looks good by me."

I handed it back to him and he lay it down onto his desk.

"It will be right here," he said, "if you need to see it, again." He tapped his fingers on it. "Well, that's pretty much it. The chores around the lodge come first. Do them in the morning when you first get here. In the afternoon, we'll work up on the slopes, together. So, go ahead and get started, work at it however you want to, just so it gets done."

"Thank you, Beck," I said.

I started out at the swimming pool. I checked the chlorine and I found it was low and added more. I cleaned the twigs out of the water with the long-handled dip net. I straightened out the chairs around the tables. I walked over to the cafeteria and I swept it and emptied the wastebaskets. I hauled the upstairs' kitchens garbage out to the burial pit. I hauled in the fireplace wood to the upstairs' lounge. I hauled wood up the slopes for the Native show. I piled it outside the lodge to build a fire out in the dance arena. At lunchtime, I met up in the cafeteria with Mr. Beck and we ate, together. We climbed up the slopes and we planted grass on the sandy spots and staked hay down over them. We walked around with snippers and we snipped off the saplings and piled them up for burning later. We walked back down the slope, together, both of us dead tired on our feet. I walked out to my car and he went back into the cafeteria. I got into it and I drove home and changed my clothes and, back up at the lodge, I waited tables in the dining room. We closed for the evening and I drove in to town and saw Jackie. She was sitting out on the front steps waiting for me. She got into the car and we drove down to Clyde's and order malts. They came, and we both sipped on them, and talked.

"I've been thinking a lot about going to college, again. If I want to go, I have the money, now. I didn't mention it to you before this, because I didn't think that I would. I didn't even think about myself, again, because I didn't think that I would."

She didn't say anything.

"People have always said to me to get all the education that I could while I was still young. Well, I've thought about it and I've decided that they're right."

She still didn't say anything.

"Is there anything that you want to say to me?"

She shook her head, no.

"Does it surprise you that I'm talking to you about it?"

"Well, actually, yeah, it does. I didn't know that you wanted to go? Or, that it was even on your mind. You never said anything to me about it, and it never occurred to me."

"Yeah, you're right. I'm sorry. I should have said something to you about it."

"Well, now you have. And now that you have, we can at least talk about it."

"Yeah, you're right, again. I'm sorry. Okay?"

She didn't say anything.

"Well, anyhow, I'll still be in town. We can still see each other."

"Yeah, we can. But we won't see as much of each other."

"Yeah, you're right. I wish that we both were going?"

"Yeah, I wish that we both were, too. But we both aren't?"

"Do you think that I should go?"

"Yeah, I do. If that's what you want for yourself. Have you thought about what you want to be?"

Yeah, I have. I want to be a lawyer, or a literature teacher. But I haven't made up my mind about it, yet. But whatever I become, I want to be my own boss. I don't want to work for somebody."

She didn't say anything.

"I've also thought about being an aeronautical engineering. I've always loved airplanes. But, I'd have to work for somebody, if I was."

"They all sound like they're a good fit for you?"

"Yeah, they do to me, too. But the bottom line about any of them is that I need a college education. When I look at it like that, it's kind of like the answer to my whole life."

"You have been doing a lot of thinking, haven't you?"

"Yeah, I guess I have, eh?"

"Yeah, you have, and I'm glad that you have, too. Someday, it could mean a lot to us, that you did."

I leaned over and I kissed her.

"The more I think about it, the more excited about it I get."

She didn't say anything.

"Classes start in six weeks."

She looked off at the river.

We kissed and hugged and she lay back down onto the seat. I got in between her legs and I put my hand up in under her shirt and fondled her tits. I went down into her panties and down around and under her butt and I felt something. I pulled it back. But I went back down to it and I felt it, again. It was a little ball of shit caught up in her hairs. The guys at school called them dingle-berries. I pulled my hand back again, and I pushed myself back up with my arms and I pulled her trousers down and off her legs and I pushed mine down and off mine and I lay back down in between hers and did it to her. I heard the little whimpers and cries and I pushed myself back up with my arms and I looked down beneath me at where I knew she was lying in the dark.

"Jackie, are you okay?"

She didn't say anything.

I lay back down on her and I squirted in her and got off.

CHAPTER 37

MR. BECK WAS OFF WORK AGAIN MONDAY. I WORKED UP on the slopes alone. I worried that I would get Jackie pregnant. That even after promising me that she wouldn't she would talk to me about marriage and family. My school friends were staying away from girls. They wanted to get an education for themselves, first. They were planning on going off to big-name universities. They were taking academic courses to prepare themselves. They were looking forward to studying law, medicine and engineering. They walked the halls with their heads held high. I wanted to be like them. I tried to imagine Clarence on the seat of a car doing it to a girl and when I couldn't do it I regretted doing it to Jackie there. I worried that I would her pregnant. That I would get tied down with her. That my friends would go off to college and leave me behind. I decided that she needed somebody with a good job that wanted to get married and start a family. I couldn't afford to get married and to go to college both. Our futures together were still too far off. There were the things that I didn't like about her, too. Like that little ball of shit that I found caught up in her hairs. She was barely five feet tall. Her butt was too flat and her boobs too big. She wore a false tooth that moved when she talked to you, sometimes. In the fall my friends would want to meet her. I worried that they would look at her and wonder what I saw. I worked hard and the sweat ran down off my forehead and into my eyes. I could barely see to do my work. After work instead of driving in to town and seeing Jackie, I stopped at home. I ate supper with my mom and my sister and drove down to Monocle Lake. The water in it was always warm. The trees blocked out the wind. They held in the sun's heat. I fished off the docks and I swam along the shore. I caught a half dozen fish off them and I took them back home with me. I cleaned them and I cooked them and ate them all myself. I went out into the living room and I lay down on the couch and watched the evening news.

I stayed, and I slept there.

In the morning I drove up to the lodge and did my morning chores out around the pool. In the afternoon Mr. Beck and I climbed up on the beginner's slope and cut the brush off it. In the evening I waited tables in the dining room and after we closed, I drove in to town. I picked up Jackie and we drove down to Clyde's and order malted milks. They came, and we both sipped on them, and talked.

"I've been worrying about getting you pregnant," I said, blurting it out. "I think about it when I'm working up on the slopes."

She said nothing. I thought that she looked confused. I asked her what she thought about it and she still said nothing.

Then, she said, "Cortney, I love you," blurting it out, too.

"I love you, too, Jackie," I said. I was confused, now, too. I wasn't sure what to say back to her, either. I already knew that she loved me. I reached out for her and she leaned into me and I held her and kissed her. I began to take off my clothes. I helped her lie back down onto the seat. She began to take off hers, too. I got in between her legs and I began doing it to her. But realizing what I was doing and who I was doing it too I stopped and, after I savored the moment, I began doing it to her, again. She whimpered and cried but I didn't stop. I kept doing it to her and I squirted in her and got back off.

"I'm sorry," I said, "for doing it to you, again."

She didn't say anything.

I watched her put her clothes back on. What we were doing wasn't making sense to me anymore. I wondered if it still was to her. We drove back to her house and we parked out front and went into it. Willis was sitting on his mother's lap. She was rocking him in his chair. They were watching tv, together. We sat down and we watched it, too. Shortly Armand got up, and went into his bedroom. Willis got up and he followed him into it. Bunny stayed behind with us and we watched another sitcom, together.

After it she left for the bar.

"I got paid again."

"Oh, uh-huh?"

"Yeah, I made five hundred dollars, again."

She didn't say anything.

"I paid off the car and some of it I'm saving up. The rest I'm going to use for gas and things."

She didn't say anything.

"Next week I'm going to put almost all of it in the bank. I should have fifteen hundred dollars saved up by then. That's enough to get me started and, if I keep working, I should have enough money to keep going. If I need to, I can get a student loan. So, money shouldn't be the problem for me that I thought it was going be, after all. Things are really starting to look up."

"Yeah, it sounds like it."

"School starts next week."

"Yeah, unfortunately it does."

"It sounds like you don't want it to?"

"No, actually, I don't. I dread the thought of it."

"Oh, you do?"

"Yeah, I do?"

"That's funny? Because I didn't like school, either. I barely managed to drag myself through it. But I think that college will be different. For one thing, I won't have to take academic classes, anymore. For another, I can get a job with what I learn, now. But the biggest difference is that there won't be anybody there who doesn't want to be. So, discipline shouldn't be the problem that it was in high school, either. Those three things together should make a real difference."

"Yeah, they should. I wish that I could get a job with what I learn. High School seems like a waste of time."

"Yeah, it did to me, too. I wondered why I even bothered to go. I'm glad that I don't have to go through that, again. Now I can study whatever I want to, too. If I don't want to, I don't even have to go to class."

Her eyes got big. "Wow, Cortney, you're so lucky," she said. "I wish that I didn't have to go to my classes."

We heard a noise at the door. We looked over at it, and Bunny was coming in it. She closed it behind herself and she walked across to us.

"I see you kids are still up?"

We smelled the beer on her breath.

Jackie shifted about, and moved away from me.

"Mom, we're watching a movie."

"Jackie, if you asked me to, I could name off a hundred movies for you right now. What do you think that I was doing night after night when I was up with you changing your diapers and feeding you your bottles? I was watching the movies. I watched a thousand of them, if I watched one. What did I learn? I learned that they're all basically alike. You watch one and you have essentially watched them all." She looked at the tv. "Jackie, I'm happy to see you and Cortney in love. I was in love when I was your age. I hope that things work out for you Well okay, that's enough out of me. I'm going upstairs to bed. But let me say this one last thing before I do. Jackie, our lives here on earth are full of disasters. No one escapes them. So, use your time wisely while you're here. If you do, you will be successful at whatever you attempt. And, if by when you' get to be my age and you're still as happy as you are now, then you can consider yourself as one of the luckier ones. Well okay, that's enough from me. I'm going upstairs to bed."

She walked off to the hallway into kitchen. But before she went into it she stopped and looked back at us.

She saw the smile on Jackie's face.

"Sure, Jackie, smile. Think that you're so smart. But by when you get to be my age, girl, you'll remember what I said to you and after you do, you won't think that you're so smart, anymore. Then, you will want to thank me for it. But by then, Jackie, I won't still be here. I'll be dead and buried, somewhere? Who will you smirk at, then?"

"Mom, we don't want to listen to that talk."

"That talk, nothing. I don't talk this way to you very often. So, don't make me out to be a monster because Cortney is here.

What I said to you about using your time wisely, I said it to help you. You're barely fifteen years old, Jackie. You're just starting out in life. You still have a lot to learn about being a woman."

"Mom, we're trying to watch this movie?"

"So, watch it? Who's stopping you, Jackie? Well, okay, that's enough out of me. I'm going upstairs to bed. But, before I do, I want to say this one last thing. Okay?"

Jackie stuck her fingers into her ears.

"Sure, stick your fingers into your ears. Block me out. Make me out to be the crazy one. When it's actually the people like yourself, who are the real crazies."

She went off into the hallway. Shortly we heard her climbing the stairs.

Jackie sat back over by me.

"She goes out drinking and she comes home and talks, like that. She's my mother but she makes me sick to my stomach, sometimes."

"My Dad goes out drinking and he comes home and talks, like that, too. I ignore him. But not my mother. She always asks him 'who's doing the talking, you or the alcohol?'" He ignores her, and he goes off upstairs."

"When my Mom's not drinking she's a whole different person. I wish that she would quit doing it, altogether."

"Yeah, it's gotten to be a problem for her?"

"Yeah, it has. But she doesn't think so. She still thinks that we're the problem around here."

"You should move out."

"Yeah, I wish that I could. But where would I move to?"

"That's the hard part, eh?"

"Yeah, it sure is," she said.

I put my arm around her.

"Jackie, I love you."

"I love you too, Cortney."

We watched the rest of the movie, sitting close. We got up and we walked out to the door, together. Out side it, we kissed and hugged and we said good night out in the cold dark.

"Goodbye, Sweetheart."

"Did you mean, goodnight?"

"Yeah, I meant to say good-night."

"It sounded so final?"

"Sweetheart, I'm sorry. It was a slip."

She said nothing.

"Sweetheart, I truly do love you. I'm never leaving you. Not for all the money in the world."

"I truly do love you, too."

We kissed and hugged, again.

"I'll see you later, then. Okay, Sweetheart?"

"Yeah, okay. I'll see you," she said.

She went back inside, and I walked out to the car. As I drove home I thought back over what we said. I did think about leaving her. I thought that she needed someone with a good job who wanted to get married and start a family. But I never said a word to her about it. But still here she was worrying that I was going to leave her. I wasn't going to leave her. I loved her too much. I wasn't ever going to go anywhere without her. I would have to run off to South America or off to Africa or off to some other place so far away that I would never see her, ever again.

CHAPTER 38

I CALLED HER FROM WORK.

"Hello."

"Hi, Sweetheart…"

"Hi, Cortney…"

"Well, what's new, today?"

"Not much is."

"Not much is out here, either."

"Mom's cranky with a hangover."

"Yeah, I suppose, eh?"

"Ellie and I are walking downtown, later."

"Oh?"

"Yeah, I'm going to lay a skirt away and she's going to buy a blouse."

"That's a good idea. Getting ready for school, eh?"

"Yeah, I still need a few things. Willis is anxious to start kindergarten."

"Oh, how's that?"

"Well, he keeps asking me if this is the morning. I keep telling him that no, that it's still this many days, away. He asked me again this morning."

"He can sure wear a person out, eh?"

"Yeah, he sure can."

"My Dad is supposed to come home this weekend. But he's not sure about it, yet. He's going to call again tomorrow."

"Oh, uh-huh?"

"Yeah, he hasn't been home since the fourth. If he can't get the time off, he's coming home Labor Day Weekend."

"That's in two weeks, eh?"

"Yeah, it is. If he waits until then he can stay a day longer. But whenever he comes home he's going to stay for at least a week.

He's saved up a lot of vacation time and he wants to use some of it up."

"Well, that's good."

"Oh, yeah? Well, that's about it for out here at home. Up here at work nothing is new."

"Oh, uh-huh?"

"Yeah, it's been really quiet."

She didn't say anything.

"Well, Sweetheart, I'm going to say good bye."

"You mean 'so long' don't you?"

"Yeah, I do, Sweetheart. I'm sorry."

"That's okay. I love you, Cortney."

"I love you, too, Jackie."

We both hung up.

I called her again Friday. We didn't talk long then, either. We tried to talk longer on Saturday and Sunday. But we didn't do much better. After work Monday I drove in to town and saw her. She was sitting out on the front steps waiting for me. She walked out to the car and she got into it with me. We drove down to Clyde's and we ordered hamburgers and cokes. They came and we both ate, and talked.

"How was your first day of school?"

"It was okay."

"How far do you have to walk?"

"It's almost seven blocks."

"That's not too far, eh?"

"No, it's not. But it will be in the winter, or if it rains."

"Yeah, I can imagine, eh?"

"Willis didn't like his first day?"

"Oh, he didn't?"

"No, he didn't like it; not at all."

"I thought that he was anxious to go?"

"Well, he was, until he got there."

"But he didn't like it, eh?"

"No, he didn't. He said that the other kids were mean to him. That they pulled his hair, and pushed him down."

"Wow, they really did, eh?"

"Yeah, I guess so. His shirt is torn."

"I bet your mom was upset?"

"Yeah, she was. But not as much as Dad was."

"Oh, yeah?"

"Yeah, he's the one that usually stays calm. But he got really upset. He couldn't understand Will's having such a hard time of it on his first day. Now, he doesn't want to go back?"

"Oh, wow?"

"Yeah, oh wow, for sure. But Dad says that he's going. So, I imagine he is."

"Yeah, it doesn't sound like he has a choice."

"No, he doesn't. But he'll think of a reason not to. He'll pretend to be sick, or something."

"Yeah, knowing Willis, I imagine he will. He'll find some excuse to stay home."

We both chuckled.

She stopped herself. "Actually," she said, "I shouldn't be laughing. I didn't tell you something. He passed out in school."

"Wow, you're kidding me?"

"No, I'm not. But I wish that I was. Because it sounds like it could be serious? The school nurse called mom and told her that they had trouble bringing him around. That they had to splash cold water into his face. She asked her if he ever passed out at home and Mom told her that he did, and about taking him down to see the doctor. She told her about the anxiety medication that he prescribed for him. Now they think that it could be his anxiety over starting school. He has an appointment to see the school psychologist."

"Well, that's good. Because it could be his nerves. But actually it could be almost anything; high blood pressure, a brain tumor, or a dozen other things?"

"Yeah, it could?"

"But let's hope that it's only his nerves, eh?"

"Yeah, that's for sure," she said.

I took a bite of my hamburger. I washed it down with my pop. When I looked back at her she was staring at me.

"I have something else to tell you, too."

"Oh, you do?"

"Yeah, I do. But promise me first that you won't get upset?"

"Oh, wow, what is it? Did I do something wrong?"

"No, you didn't? But it is serious."

"Apparently, it is. I haven't seen you look this stern, before."

"Well, I should have said that it could be serious. Because it could be nothing at all…"

"Oh, really?"

"Yeah, let's hope that it's nothing. But don't get upset, if it isn't? Okay?"

"Yeah, okay? But please hurry and tell me, or I will?"

"Okay, but promise me first that you won't? Okay?"

"Yeah, okay, I won't. Now please tell me."

"I'm overdue," she said.

"What does that mean, 'you're overdue?'"

"You don't know what that means?"

"No, I guess not?"

"Well, I guess the best way to explain it is; it's the end of the month, and I'm overdue."

"Oh, that kind of overdue? How much are you overdue?"

"Five days."

"Oh, five days, eh?"

"Yeah…? That's why I said it could be nothing."

"Well, when is it something?"

"After six days, it is. After seven days it's almost for sure."

"Well, it certainly makes you stop and think, anyway."

"Yeah, it does."

"I never thought this would happen to us, did you?"

"No, I didn't?"

"What happens if you are?"

She didn't say anything.

"I mean of course we'll get married. But what about until then; or until after then or whatever?"

"Well, let's wait and see, first, okay?"

"Yeah, okay, you're right?"

"It could be for some other reason other than, you know? Anyway, I'm taking a hot bath tonight. I read somewhere that it will help you start, if you're not?"

"That's good?"

"Yeah, maybe by when you call tomorrow everything will be okay?"

"Yeah, let's hope so? I guess there's nothing that we can do about it, except wait, eh?"

"No, I guess not?" she said.

My hamburger didn't taste as good, now. We did it three times and now this: she might be pregnant? The more I thought about it the more unbelievable it got. I remembered all the times that Delores and I did it, and she didn't get pregnant? What about my plans for going to college? What would to become of them? I would need to find a better paying job. We would need to put a deposit down on an apartment? Why, I thought, was this even happening to me? Maybe when I wake up tomorrow, boom, it's all over. She's not pregnant, I don't need a better paying job, I am still going to college.

It was all a bad dream.

"What are you thinking about?"

"Huh?"

"What are you thinking about?"

"Oh nothing? I was just thinking."

"Well, stop thinking, okay?"

"Yeah, okay?"

"I shouldn't have told you, yet."

"No, I'm glad that you did."

"Well, I could have waited until I was sure."

"No, I'm glad that you told me."

"Well, alright. But don't think about it anymore. Okay?"

"Okay. I'll try not to."

"Thanks."

"Are you done eating?"

"Yeah, I am."

I began to think about it, again.

"You're thinking about it again, aren't you?"

I didn't say anything.

"That's okay. Go ahead and think about it. I guess there's nothing that I can do about it."

"No, I guess not," I said.

I felt my face turn red. I thought of a question to ask.

"Would you like to go out to a movie, tonight?"

"Yeah, actually I would. What's the name of it?"

"Anatomy of a Murder. It was made up in Marquette."

"Oh uh-huh? I've heard about it."

"You want to go and see it, then?"

"Yeah, I do. There aren't many movies made up in the U.P. It should be good, if only for that reason, alone."

"Yeah, it should. Well, we're going, then?"

"Yeah, we are. I really want to see it," she said.

CHAPTER 39

WE DROVE DOWNTOWN TO THE SOO THEATER AND WE parked around back and walked back around to the front. We went into the lobby and we bought tickets and popcorn and pop. We took them into the auditorium and we sat down near the front. We snacked on them as we watched the cartoons. The movie started and it drew us both into it. It was about this Air Force couple stationed up at the K.I. Sawyer Air Force Base outside of Marquette. The wife liked to go out to the bars in the evenings alone. She drank all one evening with a stranger and when he offered her a ride home she accepted it. He walked her out to his car. He opened her door for her and she got into it. He closed it behind her and he walked around to his side and got into it. They drove across town to her place. They stopped out front and when she went to get out he grabbed her and he raped her. She got out and she ran into the house and she told her husband what happened. He ran off in a rage out to his car and he got into it and he drove down to the bar and he went inside, and shot the man off his bar stool. He called the sheriff and he turned himself in to him. The opening scene showed the rape. The rest was about the murder trial held up in Michigan's remote Upper Peninsula. The State Attorney General's Office sent up a high-powered prosecution team. It went up against one of Marquette County's two trail lawyers. The county's lawyer poked fun at the big-city fancy ways of the state's high-powered prosecution team. The jury came over to his side and the trial ended when his client got off on an insanity plea.

We walked back up the aisle, together.

"Well, did you like the movie?"

"Yeah, I did. It was good to see a movie made up in the U.P. I liked the storyline of it, too. But I didn't like the way that it ended. They went through so much together and still in the end they separated. I found that hard to understand."

"Yeah, I did, too. He went, and he shot the guy for her and he got away with it. But still in the end they separated. It didn't make a lot of sense to me, either."

She didn't say anything.

"But, I guess, that life doesn't always make sense, eh?"

"No, I guess not," she said.

We walked back out into the lobby, together. We walked back through it and we went back out the door and back out around the theater. We got back into our car and we got back out onto Ashmun and drove down to Portage. We turned off onto it and we drove down to Barbeau and turned off onto it. We parked out front of her house and we got out and went inside. We sat down on the couch and watched a sitcom, together.

"Did your Dad make it home, alright?"

"No, actually he didn't."

"Oh, what happened?"

"He couldn't get the time off."

"Oh, uh-huh?"

"Yeah. So, now he's coming next weekend, instead."

We both went to sleep watching tv. I woke back up first and I woke her back up. We got up and we walked out to the door, together. Outside it, we kissed and hugged out in the sparkling starlight and we said goodnight. She went back in and I walked back out to the car. I got back into it and I drove out to the highway and I pushed the gas pedal down to the floor and I held it and, watching the speedometer needle sweep up to eighty, I sped up the hill and over the top of it and, boom, I almost hit the back of another car. I hit the brakes, I skidded sideways, I jerked the steering wheel hard to the right, I let off on the brakes, I shot up alongside it and, pushing the gas pedal back down to the floor and holding it, throwing gravel everywhere, I got back over onto the blacktop and I sped off down into the valley and up the next hill and over the top of it and when I got out to Six Mile Road I turned off onto it and started out through the farming country looking ahead at Iroquois Mountain and keeping to the left I went down Hunter's

Hill and I sped off up through the cedar swamps and the birch and balsam ridges up along Lake Superior and around the corners and up-and-down over the bumps and down-and-up over the holes and I drove out through the Bay Mill's Indian Community looking out at their tarpaper shacks remembering about the Indian kids getting on the bus and being pushed up and down the aisle because the stunk and, recalling the saw wooden look on their brown Indian faces I drove up pass the Iroquois Lighthouse and I went still further up into Iroquois Beach where I turned up into the driveway and parked up by the house. I got out and I went inside and went upstairs to bed and off to sleep. In the morning I got up and my Mom and I ate breakfast, together. I walked out to the car as she picked up the dishes. I got into it and I drove up to the lodge and reported for work.

I called Jackie during coffee.

"Hello."

"Hi, Sweetheart."

"Hi."

"Is there any news, yet?"

"No, there isn't."

"Oh, okay?"

"Are you sure it's okay, Cortney?"

"Yeah, Sweetheart. Of course, I am."

"I love you, Cortney."

"I love you, too, Jackie."

We both hung up.

Chet was having a cup of coffee in the cafeteria, too. I stopped at his table on the way back from using the phone. He asked me about the car and I told him how it was running. He asked me about Jackie and me and I told him what was going on with us. "Some girls are an expensive piece of ass," he said, and laughed. I took offense to it and I said, 'talk you later' and I got back up and walked back to my own table.

CHAPTER 40

I DROVE IN AFTER WORK, AND SAW JACKIE. THERE STILL wasn't any news. The movie Bambi was playing downtown. I asked her if she wanted to go and see it. She said that she did. That although she saw it before she would like to see it, again. That it would help her get her mind off things. We drove downtown to the Soo Theater. We parked around back and we walked back around front. We went into the lobby and we bought tickets and popcorn and pop for ourselves. We took them down into the auditorium and we sat down near the front. As we snacked on them we watched the cartoons. The movie started and it drew us both into it. She saw it before, but she enjoyed seeing it, again. We got back up after it and we walked back up the aisle, together. We went back out through the lobby and we walked back out around the theater. We got back into our car and we got back out onto Ashmun and drove down to Portage. We turned off onto it and we drove up to the West Pier Drive-in. We parked and we ordered hotdogs and cokes. They came, and we pulled up by the Canal to eat.

We both ate, and talked.

"Did Willis go to school, today?"

"Yeah, he did."

"Good for your Dad? It's best that he goes, eh?"

"Yeah it is. He's going again tomorrow, too."

"Poor, Willis, eh?"

"Yeah, that's for sure?"

"He probably should be held back a year?"

"Yeah, he probably should. It wouldn't hurt him any?"

"No, it wouldn't? But we can't really know about some things, eh?"

"Yeah, that's for sure. Nobody can?"

There were cars across the river moving both ways along it. The lights on them, those on the ships, both docked and underway;

the lights on the waterfront buildings, the piers, the buoys, the television and the radio towers, blinked wherever we looked. The harbor was sparkling with them. They were numberless. I looked for some order to them, but I didn't see any.

I rolled down my window.

"Is that too cold on you?"

"Yeah, it is a little."

I rolled it back up. We watched a ship come down the Canal. It turned in to the pier and it eased itself in against it. It rubbed the fender timbers as it came down it toward us. Smoke rose up from them as it went by us and in behind a railroad bridge. We finished eating and we drove back down Portage and turned off onto Barbeau. We parked out front of her house.

We sat in the car, and talked.

"I'm really tired again, tonight."

She didn't say anything.

"I wore myself out working up on the slopes, again. I should go home and go to bed, and get some sleep."

"Are you sure that's all it is, Cortney?"

"Yes, Sweetheart, of course, I'm sure."

"I'm sorry, but I worry about us."

"Sweetheart, don't worry about us. Okay? I misspoke when I said goodbye to you. I'm not going to leave you. I love you with all my heart. I'd have run off to God knows where so that I would never see you, ever again."

"I'm sorry. I shouldn't have said that."

"That's okay. But don't worry about us, anymore. Okay?"

"Okay, I'll try not to."

"I'm sorry, if I upset you."

"That's, okay. You can go now, if you want to?"

"Yeah, I think I better. I have to get up early again."

We got out of the car.

"You're worrying about us, again, aren't you?"

"Yeah, I am sorry. I am a little."

"No, that's okay. But please try not to, okay?"

"Okay, I'll try."

I didn't say anything.

We went out the door and we stood outside it.

"Sweetheart, I love you with all my heart. Remember that when you start to worry about us, again. Okay?"

"I love you with all my heart, too, Cortney."

We kissed and hugged and we said goodnight. She went in and I walked back out to the car. As I drove for home I thought back about what we said. I did think about leaving her. But I didn't think about it, since. As I drove by my friend's house I noticed that his lights were still on. I turned around and I went back. I pulled up into the driveway and I parked up by the house. I got out and I walked up to the door.

I knocked on it and he opened it.

"Hey Cortney," he said, "it's good to see you, again." He stuck out his hand and I took it and we both shook, and smiled. "Hey, I'm glad that you stopped in. How are you doing, anyway? Let's go into the living room, and sit down and I'll get us something to drink. It's been a long time. We have a lot to talk about. Can I get you a cup of coffee, or maybe a can of pop?"

"Yeah, thanks, Clarence. A can of pop sounds good?"

He got two cokes out of the kitchen.

He gave one to me. "Thank you."

"We haven't seen each other since school," he said. "It's been over a year, now."

"Yeah, it has. I saw your lights still on as I was driving by. I decided to stop in and to take a chance that you were still up. So, how about yourself, Clarence? How is your summer going?"

"My summer's going good, Cortney. Early in it I went on a canoe trip with a friend. Later I stayed with another friend out at his cabin on Monocle Lake. Lately, I've been helping my neighbor with his haying. Other than for that and some reading I haven't done much of anything. Hey Cortney, thanks again for stopping in. I was thinking about you yesterday. Wondering if I would see you up at the college this fall. So, what's been going on with you?"

"Well, I'm working up at the resort, now. That's the biggest thing that's been going on with me. I'm waiting tables up there, and helping with the maintenance work. Other than for that, there hasn't been much going on with me, either. Oh, I didn't tell you about my girlfriend in town. That's where I'm coming back from, tonight. We went out to a show, earlier. I didn't tell you about my car, either. I finally bought a car for myself."

I saw him staring at me.

"Cortney," he said, "you know that they're trained to get the best of you? Give them half a chance to do it and they will, too. Just when you think everything is going okay, boom, she's pregnant. There's a baby on the way and you're making plans to get married."

"Yeah, I know all about that stuff, Clarence. I see it happening to a lot of guys, all the time. But rest assured, it's not going to happen to me."

"Well, I certainly hope not, Cortney." He sat back on the couch as if to think. "Well, what about college this fall? Am I going to see you up there? Classes start in three weeks."

"Yeah, you probably will. I have a car and the money to go, now. So yeah, you'll probably see me, up there?"

"Good. I was hoping that I would. I was surprised when I didn't see you up there, last year."

"You're a sophomore now, eh?"

"Yeah, I am. My freshman year went by fast. I lost track of time and before I knew it, I was a sophomore."

We talked about his freshman year. All the courses that he took were prerequisites. I would be taking them, too. Now he was taking pre-law courses. Before the end of the semester he hoped to be enrolled in the Cooley School of law. I told him about my interest in studying law, too.

He got up, and got us another coke.

"So," he said, handing it to me, "you're waiting tables up at the resort, now? You were lucky to find something close to home."

"Yeah, I was."

He looked at the tv.

"When you stopped in I was watching Sixty Minutes. They're talking about the arms race. They're comparing our number of ballistic missiles with Russia and China's. I think it's something that you would be interested in watching. We can both watch it, and talk too, if you want to?"

"Yeah, I would. I've always liked watching Sixty Minutes. I watch it a lot. It's a really good program."

"Do you watch a lot of tv?"

"No, I don't. But, I do, if I have the time to."

"You learn a lot about things. I try to watch it every week. I always learn something new, whenever I do."

"Yeah, I do, too."

"Well Cortney, what else is new?"

"Actually Clarence, very little else is new. I told you about my girlfriend in town and my car, and job. That's pretty much it, for me."

"Well, I'm glad to hear about your plans for college. I was hoping that I would see you up there this fall. You're definitely college material. That's a good head you got on those shoulders."

"Thank you, Clarence. I appreciate hearing you say that."

He smiled at me.

"So, you bought a car for yourself? What kind did you get?"

"It's a '04' Ford Mustang. I paid a guy up at work twenty-seven hundred and fifty for it. It has a big V-8 in it. You kick it into overdrive and it does eighty in second gear."

"So, you are having yourself a good summer?"

""Yeah, I guess I am, eh?"

"Yeah, it sounds like it to me."

"You can look at it before I go, if you want to?

He stared at me, again.

"Cortney, don't get too serious about her right away? Okay? Don't get ahead of yourself. There will be lots of time for that stuff, later. After you graduate with that engineering degree."

"Yeah, I know, Clarence. I've been thinking about that. The last thing that I want to do is get her pregnant. I'm taking it real slow. I can't afford to get married, or any of that stuff."

"Well, you have to take it slow? Remember they're trained to get the best of you. Give them half a chance to do it, and they will, too. You can't afford to get married and to go to college, both."

I smiled a little. I didn't feel like talking about it, anymore. He smiled a little, himself. I sensed that he still wanted to. I sat back on the couch by him. We both shrugged a little, and chuckled.

"They all sound like they're a good fit for you," he said. "You've always loved airplanes, and wanted to work around them. So, I'm not surprised by that. You have always wanted to study law too, and have your own law office, someday. So, I'm not surprised by that, either. But, what about writing? I can't remember you wanting to write?"

"Well, Clarence, remember literature class? Remember all the poems that we wrote for it? Well, I'm still writing them, today. I've been writing them ever since taking that class."

"Yeah, I remember you reading them to us," he said.

He got up, and turned down the tv.

"Yeah, I wouldn't have to work for somebody, if I was a writer. I could be my own boss. That's what I like most about it. It's the same thing with being a lawyer. But, yeah, if I was an engineer, I would have to work for somebody. But the thing about that is, is that I would be working around airplanes. That, at least to some degree, would make up for it."

Clarence went on alone from there. He talked about the threat posed to world peace by the nuclear armed dictatorships, like Iran and North Korea. He wondered if in today's world the United States could still afford to be a world superpower. He liked the idea of a presidential triumvirate leading our nation, rather than a single individual. He thought that it would do a better job of representing the people. Tonight, I noticed something was different about him. He always had this leadership aura about him. It drew people to him. But tonight, he also had this statesman's aura. I imagined it drawing people to him, too. But Clarence always was special. In our senior year we voted him most likely to succeed. All throughout high school he was our class president. His grade point average was always the highest in the class. In his commencement speech to us he talked about the challenges ahead of our generation in an increasingly dangerous world. He thought of the Peace Corps as a symbol of America's good intentions throughout the world. Someday, he hoped to serve in it, himself.

I got up to go.

"Well, Clarence, I better get going. I need to get up early, again. Thanks for being a good host, okay? I always enjoy talking to you. I'm even more excited about starting college, now. I'm looking forward to seeing you, up there."

"Thank you, Cortney. I always enjoy talking to you, too. Stop in again, okay. But do it sooner the next time. Hey, I'm looking forward to seeing you, up there, too? That's a good head you got on those shoulders. Well, okay, I'll let you go. Stop in again. We'll catch up on things, again. Okay?"

"Yeah, okay, Clarence. I'll do that. Well, I better get back on the road. Take care of yourself, now."

"Thank you, Cortney. Drive carefully on the way home."

"Thank you, Clarence, I will."

I let myself back out the door. I walked back out to the car. I got back into it and I got back out onto the road. As I started off down it I felt myself swelling up with pride. I was going to be a college man, after all. I imagined myself sitting in the college library and reading a novel and preparing to discuss it in class the next day. I thought about the baby on its way. I imagined myself standing in a clothes hanger factory at a plastic injection molding machine and struggling against an impulse to quit and walk out. I wished that Jackie would hurry and start her period. I wanted my life back. I pushed the gas pedal down to the floor and I held it and I went up the hill feeling pulled down into my seat and I went up and over the top of it feeling it fall out from under me and I went down it and through the valley and up the next hill feeling pulled down into it and up and over the top of it feeling it fall out from under me.

CHAPTER 41

I GOT UP IN THE MORNING AND I ATE BREAKFAST WITH MY
Mom. I walked out to the car and I drove up to the lodge. I checked
the chlorine in the pool and I straightened out the chairs around
the tables. I walked over to the cafeteria and I drank a cup of coffee
with Mr. Beck.

I called Jackie.

"Hello."

"Hi, Sweetheart..."

"Hi..."

"Is there any news, yet?"

"No, nothing, yet."

I sighed a little. "Sorry, Honey?"

"That's okay?"

"I'll come in after work and see you, okay? We will go for a
ride, somewhere?"

"Yeah, okay."

"Okay, I'll see you later."

"Bye, I love you."

"Bye, I love you, too."

We both hung up.

I swept out the cafeteria and emptied the wastebaskets. I
hauled the upstairs' kitchen garbage out to the burial pit. I met
up in the cafeteria with Mr. Beck and we ate lunch. We sat and we
visited over a cup of coffee. I told him about my plans for college.
He said that his son went to college, up there. That he studied civil
engineering. That after he graduated he got himself a good paying
job with a big construction outfit. I asked him if he stayed in the
college dorm, or if he rented a room nearby.

"Well, actually he didn't do either one," he said. "He was
married at the time. They stayed up there in those married housing apartments."

"Oh, how long ago was that?"

"Oh, I don't rightly remember how long ago that was. It wasn't that long ago? Maybe six or seven years have passed since then."

"I've never heard of married housing apartments? What was their rent?"

"Oh, I don't rightly remember what it was, anymore. Three hundred dollars I think it was. It was low, at any rate. But they weren't much in the way of apartments, either. Just what the military left behind from when they owned that place, up there. They called them non-commissioned officer quarters. NCOs' with their families lived in them. They weren't anything like what they got up there, now."

"Oh?"

"Yeah, they looked more like a barracks. That place up there used to be the old Fort Brady, you know, before the college took it over? They were nice enough in the way of apartments for the money. I was in theirs a couple times when I went up for a visit."

"I might be renting one."

"Oh, how's that? You're not married, are you?"

"No, I'm not, now. But I could be, by the time college starts."

"Oh, how's that? Not girl trouble, eh?"

"Actually, yeah? I think so?"

"Well, I'll be darned? That's what got my son, up there," he said.

He wanted to know about it. I told him the whole story. We climbed up on the intermediate slope. A tree was blown down on it and we cut it up into firewood. We hauled it down and we piled it outside the lodge. I drove back home and I changed my clothes and, back up at the lodge, I waited tables in the dining room. We closed and I drove in and saw Jackie.

"Hi."

"Hi."

We kissed and hugged. We walked out into the kitchen, together.

"I'm tired again, today. How about you?"

"No, I'm okay."

"I wore myself out again working up on the slopes."

She didn't say anything.

"Would you like to go out somewhere and eat?"

"No, actually I'm not hungry."

"Actually, I'm not, either."

"There's still no news."

"Oh, okay?"

"But I've thought of something that we can do, if you want to?"

"Oh, what's that?"

"We can ride the ferry over to Canada. Over there we can go for a walk."

"Yeah, that sounds fun. I'm glad that you thought of it."

"Good. We'll do it, then?"

"Yeah, you bet?" I said.

She went upstairs to get a sweater. I went out into the living room, to wait. Armand was watching the evening news. I sat down and I watched it with him.

"How are you, Armand?"

"Okay, I guess."

"I'm working lots of overtime."

"Yeah, that's what Jackie tells me."

"Yeah, I worked every day this week."

"Yeah, that's what I understand from what she says. I missed seeing you around here. She says that you're going to start at the college, up there, too?"

"Yeah, I'm hoping to. It's not a hundred percent, yet."

"Well, that's good. Get all the education that you can while you're still young. It won't hurt you any and in the end, it might help some."

"Yeah, that's what I think, too."

Jackie walked through the room. I got up and follow her out to the door.

"Armand, talk to you later, okay?"

"Yeah okay, Cortney, talk to you later," he said.

Jackie and I went out the door. We got into the car and we drove uptown and parked at the ferry dock. We went into the ticket office and we bought tickets and walked out to the ferry. We got onto it and we climbed up to the upper deck and sat down on the benches, up there. We looked around at the harbor. There were blinking lights wherever we looked. They seemed to be dancing on the water. The harbor was sparkling with them. We couldn't stop looking at them. There were cars and passengers coming aboard. The deckhand pulled up the loading ramp. The ferry backed away from the dock. It turned around and it went across the river. It pulled in to the dock over there. The cars and passengers got back off. Other cars and passengers came aboard. We stayed on it. The deckhand pulled up the loading ramp, again. The ferry back away from the dock, like before. It turned around and it went back across the river. It pulled back into the dock over there. We stayed on it, again. We rode it back and forth across it three more times. We got back off and we walked back out to our car. We got back out onto Portage and we drove back down to Clyde's and ordered chocolate malts'. They came, and we both sipped on them, and talked.

"I've been thinking about renting a married housing apart-ment. I have enough money to put a deposit down on one, now. And, if I keep working as I'm going, we can afford to rent it."

She didn't say anything.

"We can ride up there tomorrow and look at them, if you want to?"

She didn't say anything.

I looked in to her eyes. There were tears in them. I took her hands and I wrapped them in mine. She took hers out and she wrapped mine in hers, instead. We sat looking in to each other's eyes. Neither of us said anything. It reminded me of when I ate with her family for the first time. They stopped eating and they looked up at us whenever we said something. We began to talk with our eyes. I was amazed by what we could still say with just them.

CHAPTER 42

WE GOT BACK TO THE HOUSE AND THE LIGHTS WERE OFF. We went into it and we turned them back on. We turned on the tv and we snuggled up on the couch. We went to sleep watching, Man of the Family.

I woke up first and I woke her up.

"It's really late, Sweetheart. I need to go. Please sit up and let me by you."

She sat up and let me by her.

"I'm sorry for waking you up, Sweetheart."

"You're coming back in the morning, aren't you?"

"Yes, I am, Sweetheart. Lay back down and go back to sleep."

She got up, instead.

"I'll walk out to the door with you," she said.

We walked out to the door, together. Outside it, we kissed and hugged out in the moonlight and we said goodnight. She went back inside, and I walked out to the car. I got into it and I headed for home. I was driving by the old depot when the radio announcer said it was 3:00 a.m. I turned around and I drove back and parked in around behind it. I lay down on the seat but I couldn't stop thinking about Jackie and couldn't go to sleep. I opened my eyes again and it was daybreak, now. I got up still feeling tired. I rolled down the window and I let in fresh air. I got the car back out onto the street and I drove back in and saw Jackie.

She opened the door.

"Hi."

"Hi," I said.

We kissed and hugged.

"I got up feeling tired, again."

"Oh, how come?"

"I pulled in around behind the old depot and I slept in the car. Or I should say that I tried to sleep in it. I couldn't get comfortable and I couldn't go to sleep. I opened my eyes again and it was daybreak."

She didn't say anything.

"I think we need to slow down."

"Yeah, I think we do, too."

We walked out into the kitchen, together. I sat down at the table and she sat down on my lap. I wrapped my arms around her and I felt for a bulge in her tummy. But I didn't feel one.

"If you want to, we can ride up to the college, and look at the apartments, today?"

"Yeah, I do."

"Classes start in two weeks."

"Yeah, uh-huh."

"We have a million things to do, by then?"

"Yeah, we do?"

"We have to get married."

"Yeah…"

"That by itself is a lot to think about, eh?"

"Yeah, it sure is."

"We have to put a deposit down on an apartment."

"Yeah, uh-huh."

"If you miss school, what will your Mom say?"

"She won't say anything, because I won't tell her."

We both chuckled a little.

We drove up to the college and we rode around what was the old Fort Brady's parade ground. We passed by the auditorium and the fine arts' building and the book store. We pulled into the administration building and we parked and got out. We went in to it and we walked up to the information desk and asked about married housing. The woman told us about it and she gave us a key into one. We walked back across the lobby and we went back out the door and started across campus. We went past the gymnasium, the fine art's building and the book store again. We came to a long row of small wooden houses. We stopped and we looked around for a building that looked like an old army barracks. When we didn't see one we matched the number on key to one of the small houses. We walked over to it and we unlocked the door and went into it. We stood and we looked around at it. It was big for how small it looked from the outside. We liked the way that it was laid out and decorated. We decided that we wanted to rent it. We went back out and we walked back across campus and went back into the administration building. We told the woman at the information counter that we wanted to rent it. We put a hundred dollars down on it. She smiled happily at us and we smiled happily back at her. She handed the receipt to Jackie and she folded it and put it into her purse.

"Let's celebrate with a coke down at Woolworth's," I said.

We walked back out to the car and we drove down to Wool Worth's and parked out front. We went into it and we walked up to the lunch counter. But before we could sit down at it she took my hand and tugged on it. She led us off into the newborns' and she found a pair of pajamas that she liked. We took them up to the cashier and we paid for them. We walked back up to the lunch counter but before we could sit down at it she took my hand and tugged on it, again. She led us off to housewares and she found a broom and a dust pan that she liked. We took them up to the cashier and we paid for them, too. We walked back up the lunch counter still again and, this time, we sat down at it and ordered cokes.

We both sipped on them, and talked.

"Jackie, you're a riot, sometimes."

"Cortney, I think we both are."

"You can be so practical?"

"It pays to be practical."

"Jackie Claire, I truly love you."

"I truly love you, too, Cortney Parish."

We kissed and hugged, and smiled.

The apartment was unfurnished. The kitchen would need pots and pans, and dishes. The bedroom would need a bed, blankets, sheets and pillows. The baby needed a crib, a pillow, blankets, sheets, pacifiers, bibs, bottles, baby wipes, diapers, pajamas and t-shirts. We talked about moving into it. We both got excited. We drank off our cokes and we walked back out to the car and drove back to her house and parked out front. We walked up to the door and we kissed and hugged out in the light of the silvery moon and we said goodnight.

"I love you with all my heart."

"I love you with all mine, too."

We kissed and hugged, again.

"Bye, Honey. I'll call you in the morning, okay?"

"Yeah, okay. Goodnight, I love you."

"Goodnight, I love you, too."

She went into the house and I walked back out to the car.

BOOK SIX

Dad's home for a visit

CHAPTER 43

IN THE AFTERNOON I WORKED UP ON THE SLOPES. I thought about Jackie as I worked. We would soon be living in our own apartment. There would be college tuition to pay. There would be textbooks to buy. We would have to watch every penny that I earned, and more. After work I went to start the car and it wouldn't start. The starter didn't engage the motor. I rocked it back and forth and started it and began the ride in to town. Halfway in I realized that she was in school. I drove over to the school and I parked out front. I went into the principals' office and I asked to have a note sent to Jackie Claire. The woman handed a notepad and pencil to me. I wrote on it for her to meet me out front. I gave it back to the woman and I went back out to my car to wait.

I saw her coming across the lawn. There was a smile on her face. She walked up to the car.

"Hi, Jackie."

"Hi."

She got in with me.

"Are you surprised to see me here?"

"Oh, I don't know? Yes and no, I guess?"

"I thought that you would be?"

"Well, truthfully, I am a little. But actually, I thought that you might come in, today."

"Oh, really? I haven't picked you up at school, before."

"Yeah, I know. But you didn't know me when I went to school."

"No, I guess not, eh?"

She was still smiling.

"You seem to be happy, today?"

"Yeah, I am," she said.

She slid across the seat to sit by me. I knew why she was happy. But I didn't say anything to her about it. She slid ahead on it, and she turned around and looked back at me.

"I have something to tell you."

I waited for her to.

I knew what it was.

"I started."

"You did what?"

"You know?"

I knew.

"Really?"

"Yeah, really?"

It was unbelievable. It was wonderful. It was amazing. It was a total riot.

"You really and truly did, eh?"

"Yeah, I truly did," she said.

I was astounded. I was overwhelmed. I was all smiles. I felt light as air. I was happy and joyous and elated.

"Wow, do I feel better."

She didn't say anything.

"Wow, I feel better, lighter, everything," I said. "I feel like a huge weight has lifted off me." I took short deep breaths and my chest heaved and sank. "Oh, my God, do I feel better."

She still didn't say anything.

I stopped talking as it dawned on me why she was quiet. We both knew now that she wasn't pregnant. That she wasn't going to have our baby. That we weren't going to get married and have a family of our own, after all. That we weren't going to have a home. That we weren't going to need the broom or the dustpan, or the baby pajamas. That they all could be taken back to Woolworth's. She moved back around on the seat by me. She slouched down on it and her chin fell down onto her chest. Our world was stopping again. It would start back up. But it would be going in the other direction, now. Our lives, together, were changing, again.

I felt embarrassed for being so relieved.

"I'm sorry for feeling so relieved."

She didn't say anything.

"I didn't realize what I was doing."

"That's okay, I understand. It's alright," she said.

I looked up the street at the bridge over the power canal. I could see it as clearly as her sitting beside me. I could count the rivets holding it, together. I never knew anything like it, before. I looked away and back at it and I could still see it as clearly as her. The street up to it, the houses up along it, the trees out front of them, they all looked close enough to reach out and touch.

I looked back at her.

"I'm sorry for drifting off."

She didn't say anything.

"Would you like to go for a ride?"

"Yeah, uh-huh, where to?"

"We can ride down along the river, if you want to?"

She smiled a little.

"I'll call work and tell them I'll be in late."

She didn't say anything.

She looked up the street at the bridge herself, now. But she didn't say anything to me about it. We drove down along the river looking out through the trees at it. We pulled into Sugar Loaf Mountain. We parked and we got out and climbed to the top. We stood and we looked up and down at the river. We didn't see a ship. We looked out across it at the mountains in Canada.

"Do you still feel that your life is too small?"

"Why are you asking me that?"

"I've been wondering about it?"

"Why?"

"Because I feel that way myself, sometimes."

"Well, truthfully, yeah, I do? I told you about riding in the airplane, eh? How afterward I wanted my life to go back to normal. How I couldn't stop thinking about how small everything looked. Well, anyway, it got to the point to where if I was playing kick-the-can out on the beach road and I looked back at the bluff, I'd think about it, again."

"Oh, uh-huh?"

"Yeah, I still feel that way, sometimes. But not as much as I did. At least it hasn't been bothering me as much."

"Things are always so complicated, eh?"

"Yeah, they sure are," I said.

It felt good to stand by her, to hold her hand and to talk to her. But shortly I was back to thinking about it, again.

"Yeah, after that plane ride I was down in the dumps. I joined the school band to keep busy, but I quit it to play basketball and then quit basketball. I wasn't doing much of anything then other than going to my classes and sitting through a long boring study hall. It got to the point to where I hated to even get up out of bed to go school. If the shop teacher didn't talk me into staying until after I graduated, I would have quit. Everybody else was doing okay and, myself, I was barely hanging in there."

She didn't say anything.

"But I'm doing better, now. I've learned to keep my mouth shut and to keep going forward, no matter what else is going on. Unless I stop, and I think about things too much, I do okay."

"It sounds like you're not happy with your life. I can say that to you because I'm not happy with mine, either. Like you, I don't like getting up in the morning and going to school, either. I'm not in band and I don't play sports and I'm not doing much of anything myself other than going to my classes and sitting through a long boring study hall, too. But being that you're a guy, I think that it's even harder on you. Whereas I can get married and I can start a family and I'm all set, you're expected to go out into the world and make something of yourself."

I didn't say anything.

"We should probably start back, eh?"

"Yeah, we probably should."

I pulled up a handful of the grass and I rolled it back and forth between my hands and I smelled it and threw it out over the river.

"It took us so long to get up here, I hate to go back down."

"Yeah, I know what you mean. But knowing my Mom, I think we better. She might call the sheriff and report us missing, or something?"

We both chuckled a little.

On the way back down the trail I thought back over what we said. It was our most serious disagreement today. Our feelings were bruised by it. I looked out across the river at the mountains in Canada. I thought back over what she said about them earlier. That they looked close enough to reach out and touch. That, I thought, she was right about. She was right about our lives being too small, too. But I was determined that they wouldn't be forever. Someday I would go to law school. I would get a juris doctorate degree and I would have a law office of my own. I would make a lot of money and I would live in a big house on a lake with my gorgeous wife and our two beautiful children. We would take long trips to Europe and visit all the famous places.

Back down at the car I put the key into the ignition and I turned it, and nothing happened. I got back out and I rocked it back and forth. I got back into it and I turned it and started it. We drove back up along the river to the Soo. We parked out front of her house and we got out and went into it. Bunny was sitting in Willis's chair with him on her lap. She was rocking him back and forth.

They were watching t v, together.

"Mom, did Willis go to school, today?"

"Yeah, Jackie, he did. But he didn't stay. They called here almost as soon as he got there. We went down and we got him and brought him back home." She picked up a letter. "They sent this letter home with him. Now they think that he's not ready for school. That he should wait until next year to start." She put it back down. "They want for all of us to go in for counseling with him. My God, I hate it when those school officials do this to us? Who in the hell do they think they are, anyway? We pay their wages. They work for us. It's not right that we should have to go in there, and tell on each other. They have no business butting into our lives, like this. It irritates the hell out of me."

Jackie smiled.

"Sure, Jackie, smile; think that you're so smart. But you'll be right in there with us, girl. You know how your Dad is about these things?"

Jackie said nothing.

I looked at her and she was looking out the window. She's probably thinking about counseling with her family, I thought. I could understand her look of concern, if she was. I wouldn't want to go in for it with my family, either. The movie ended and Willis got up off his mother's lap and went into his bedroom. Bunny got off the chair and went upstairs. Jackie and I snuggled up on the couch, together. We watched another movie and we got back up and walked out to the door. Outside it, we kissed and hugged and we said good-night out in the cold dark. She went back inside, and I walked out to my car.

CHAPTER 44

I DROVE OVER TO SPRUCE AND I TURNED OFF ONTO IT. I drove through the historic district looking out the car windows at the old homes. I stopped at the Augusta Street stop sign and I looked over at the shuttered gas station. I drove through the intersection admiring the new Super Value Store and I stopped at the Ashmun Street stop sign and I turned off onto it and drove up Ashmun Hill feeling as if I was coming back up out of a hole. There was something else going on inside me, too. But I wasn't sure what it was. I got up to the top of the hill and I looked out over the brown hayfield and the black-streaked fence posts, the rusted barbed wire still attached to them, and out beyond them to the far-off horizon of trees. I could see them as clearly as the road in front of me. I drove out to Six Mile Road and I turned off onto it and started out through the country looking at The Mission Hill ahead. I kept to the left going down Hunter's Hill and I sped up through the Bay Mills Indian Community and still further out up along Lake Superior to Iroquois Beach where I turned up into the driveway and parked up by the house. I went into it of it and I walked through the living room without saying hi to my mother or looking at her and I climbed up the stairs into my bedroom and changed my clothes. I walked back down through it without saying anything to her or looking at her again and I went back out the door and got back into my car and drove up to the lodge. I reported for work to Mr. Beck. He didn't say anything about me being late. I got home after work and my Dad was there. He was lying on the couch with one arm under his head and his other arm up over it sleeping off a drunk. I didn't know whether I should wake him up and say hello to him or to go off upstairs to bed. I went off upstairs to bed. I got up in the morning and I got dressed and went down into the kitchen. I sat down with both my Mom and Dad and we ate breakfast, together.

"Cortney, it's good to see you, again."

"Dad, it's good to see you, again, too."

We never shook hands. We didn't this morning, either.

"How's your job going?"

"It's going okay."

"Do you still like waiting tables?"

"Yeah, I do. What time did you get home?"

"Oh, I got here about three? Wasn't it Gladys?"

"Yeah, about three," my Mom said.

"What do you say we get up early, and drive up to the Naomokong, and we do some fishing, up there? Do you think you'll feel up to it?"

"Yeah, sure I will."

"Good. You work again tomorrow, eh?"

"Yeah, I do. But I don't have to be up there until noon."

"That's good. We'll have lots of time."

"Yeah, so we should be alright, eh?"

"Yeah, we should. Okay, we'll get up early, and we'll get up there, and catch some fish."

"Sounds good," I said.

I got back up and I walked out to the car. I drove up to the lodge and I reported for work to Mr. Beck. We worked up on the intermediate slope, together. I drove back home and changed my clothes and, back up at the lodge, I waited tables in the dining room. Later back home upstairs, I laid awake in my bed all night thinking about Jackie.

"Cortney, you awake?"

"Huh, Dad?"

"Come on, get up. It's time to get going."

"Yeah, okay, Dad. I'll be right down."

"Come on. Your mother's got breakfast on the table."

He went back down the stairs. I got up and I got dressed and went down, now, too. I sat down at the table and I ate breakfast with them. Dad and I hauled our gear out to the car. We put it into the trunk and we got into the front. We drove up the lake shore and we parked down at the river mouth. It rained overnight. The water was high. The current was fast in the middle. We got our gear back out and we hauled it down to the bank. I baited the hook and I fed it out into the river and, as I watched it, the current took it down into the corner where it disappeared down into a swirl of water.

Dad walked up to me.

"Your mother says that you're spending all your time in town."

"Yeah, I have been. But I'm not going to, anymore."

"What does that mean?"

"Just what it sounds like: I have been but I'm not, anymore."

I didn't think that it was any of his business.

"Troubles in paradise?" he said.

"Yeah, I guess you could say that," I said.

It wasn't something that I wanted to talk about. It probably wouldn't be for some time. I felt myself tightening up and as I breathed deeply to relax a trout struck my bait. I jerked hard on the pole to set the hook, but I missed it. It struck again, and I jerked hard on it again and this time I set the hook. I held tight onto the pole as the trout came up out of the hole and out into the current and swam up it towards us.

It swam across to the other side.

"Easy does it. Easy does it, now," Dad said.

"Okay? I got it. I got it?" I said.

"Give him time. Give him time, now."

"Yeah, okay? I am, I am," I said.

It irritated me the way he always tried to take over things. The trout went swimming up the other side of the river and it turned around up there and it came swimming back down it and it went back down into the hole where I set the hook and coming back up out of it out into the current again it went swimming up past me to where it thrust itself up out of the water and up the bank's steep incline to where it scurried across it before coming back down it and splashing back down into the river.

"Wow, what a beauty," I said.

"Keep your line tight," Dad said.

"Yeah, I am, I am," I said.

It went swimming back down the river and it went back down into the hole and coming back up out of it out into the current and swimming up it toward me it went between my legs and went swimming still farther up it to where it thrust itself up out of the water and came to a stop above it, head up, tail down, before slipping back down into it and swimming back down it and going back down into the hole, again.

I leaned back on the pole and I cranked hard on the reel. My Dad reached out to take it away from me.

"I got it, I got it," I said.

"Yeah, okay? Keep your line tight."

"He's slowing down. Got the net ready?"

"It's ready? Bring him in. It's ready."

"I'm bringing him in."

"Take it easy, now. Take it easy, okay?"

Coming back up out of the hole the trout went swimming back up pass me to where my Dad was standing with the dip net and reaching out with it he scooped him up out of the river. It was a beauty of a trout. Dad got him through the gills and he hoisted him up to where we both could get a good look at him.

"He sure is a beauty, eh?"

"Yeah, he sure is," dad said.

His rainbow colors glistened in the sunlight. He lay him down on the grass and he covered him over with wet ferns. We left him there, and we walked farther up the river. Dad caught a big trout in the next corner. He lay him down on the grass and he covered him over with wet ferns, too. We left him, too, and we walked still further up the river. I caught another big trout in the next corner, too. Now we quit fishing and we walked back down along it, together. We picked up the fish along the way and we carried them back to the car with us. We put them into the trunk and we got into the front and drove back down along the lake shore. We stopped at the Ranger Road Store and we carried them inside and weighed them out. They weighed out at 27 pounds, 10 plus ounces, altogether. That first big trout was still the biggest. We weighed him out at 13 pounds, 8 plus ounces. We drove back down along the lake shore and we pulled up in to the driveway and parked up by the house. Dad carried the trout inside as I got ready for work. I drove up to the lodge and I reported to Mr. Beck. We worked up on the expert slope, together. Later, after I went back home and changed my clothes, I waited tables in the dining room and still later, back at home upstairs again, I went to bed and off to sleep. In the morning we were getting up early again. Dad was leaving back for work in Chicago. He wanted to get in as much fishing as he could before he left.

"Hey Cortney, come on, wake up."

"Yeah, okay, Dad."

"Come on. Your mother's got breakfast on the table."

He went back down the stairs. I got up and I went down them, too. We ate breakfast, together. We drove up the lake shore and we parked down at the river mouth. We got our gear out and we fished the corners, again. We caught three trout and we quit and walked back down to the car. We drove back home up along the lake shore. He carried the fish in to the house as I got ready for work, again.

I said goodbye before I left.

"Well, Dad, I got to get to work. See you the next time you get home, okay."

"Yeah, Cortney, we'll see you in October, okay? We'll get out and do some more fishing, together."

"Yeah, Dad. See you, then, okay?"

We both nodded, and smiled.

He waved to me as I got into the car. I drove out the driveway. I turned up to the lodge. I worked with Mr. Beck up on the expert slope. I got home after work and a letter was waiting on the table for me.

Dear Cortney,

I love you so much. Please come and see me. Whatever I did that you didn't like, I'm sorry for. Please let me make it up to you. I love you and miss you so much, my heart aches for you.

                                    I love you, Jackie

I nearly drove in. But I went upstairs to bed instead. Noon the next day, I drove up to work. Mr. Beck and I worked up on the expert slope. I waited tables in the dining room and, after we closed, I drove back home. There was another letter waiting on the table for me.

Dear Cortney,

     You got my letter yesterday. I waited all day hoping you would call. My heart's aching so much, Cortney. I love you and want to see you so much. Please, Please, Please, call or come, and see me. Please, once. I miss you.

                         I love you, Jackie.

I crumpled it. I went upstairs to bed. I got up before noon, again. I drove up to work and after work when I got back home another letter was waiting on the table for me.

Dear Cortney,

     When you read this I will be in school. It will be the first day since I've seen you, I've been so heart-sick. Oh, Cortney, if you only understood how I felt you would come and see me. I love you so much more than life, itself. I don't want to go on living without you. I don't think I can. Please, please call or come and see me. If you had a phone I would call you - if I could I would drive out to see you - I love you and miss you so much.

                         I love you, Jackie

I almost went in, again. I crumpled it, instead. Her words dug at me. I will always remember them clearly. No words before or since have meant as much. I got a letter from her every day for the next week. I read them only if I dared to. In October I got a letter from her every third or fourth day. She quit writing to me, altogether, in November.

CHAPTER 45

I THOUGHT THAT I WOULDN'T NEED HER. THAT I WOULD get along without her. That I would have nothing more to do with her. But I missed kissing and hugging her too much. Every time that I thought about her I was making love to her. I missed wrapping my arms around her and pulling her in tight and nuzzling the back of her neck. I was out in the hallway smoking a cigarette when I overheard these two guys talking about this Claire girl. One of them said that she was doing it with everyone. The heart nearly fell out of me. It hurt me to even think about it. Until that moment I didn't realize how much I still cared for her. I hurried to a phone and I called her up.

"Hello," she said.

"Hi, Jackie," I said.

There was a silence.

"Can I come and see you?" I said.

There was another silence.

"Yeah," she said.

"When should I come?"

"You can come Wednesday night, if you want to."

"Yeah, okay. I'll see you, then," I said.

I was going to my classes six hours a day. I was studying in the library for another eight. The admissions' officer said that before the end of the year most of us freshmen would drop out. I didn't want to be one of them. I felt whole again after I talked to her. Like I was back with someone who I was meant to be with. I was at peace with myself for the first time in a long time. After my last class I drove back home, and I sat down at the kitchen table and studied until midnight. I went to bed and I got back up at six and shortly after seven I was back on the road for the Soo. The day came for me to go and see her. I drove over to her house and I parked out front, like before.

As I knocked on the door she opened it.

"Hi, come in," she said.

There wasn't a smile on her face.

I hesitated before going in.

"Hi," I said.

"We can go out into the living room," she said.

"Would you like to go out for a hamburger, instead?" I said.

"Sure, let me get a sweater, first," she said.

She went out into the kitchen and she came back in wearing it. We walked out to the car, together.

"Any place in particular that you'd like to eat?" I said.

"No, any place is okay," she said.

"How about driving down to Clyde's?" I said.

"Sure," she said.

We drove down to Clyde's and we ordered hamburgers and cokes. We pulled up to the river to eat, like we used to.

"How have you been?" I said.

She didn't say anything.

I didn't either, now.

Our order came and we ate our hamburgers and drank our cokes. I was throwing out the wrappers when she began to talk to me. She said that she missed seeing me. That she and Ellie went up to the college dances hoping to see me, up there. I didn't know what to say back to her. She was sad about things. I bit my tongue when I felt like I needed to. She slid ahead on the seat and she turned around on it. She squared herself away to me. She started to talk to me but instead she stopped herself and sat back around by me.

"How has everyone been?" I said.

She looked off at the river.

"You haven't heard, have you? Of course, you haven't. We haven't been in touch. But Willis's problem was much more serious than we realized. They didn't know what it was until it was too late. An arrhythmic heart caused him his troubles." Her voice cracked. "He died a couple months ago." She took short deep breaths. "Mom and Dad separated soon after. Mom moved out without telling anyone that she was going. She has an apartment downtown."

I felt like I should say something.

"I'm sorry for the hurt that I caused you, Jackie," I said.

She cried hard, now. I watched her shudder. She put her hands up to her mouth. She tipped her head back and she looked out the car windshield. She stopped crying. She sobbed for a while. We drove back to her house. We didn't kiss or hug at the door, or say goodnight. She went inside, and I walked back out to the car. I called her again in the morning. I asked her if I could come and see her, again. She said that I could. I asked her when and she said tomorrow at five.

After my last class I drove over to her house, again. I knocked on the door and she opened it. We said hello. I asked her if she wanted to drive down to Clyde's and eat, again. She said that she did. We drove down to it and we ordered hamburgers and cokes. We sat and we ate them and didn't talk. We drove back up to her house. We went inside, and we sat down on the couch and put our hands into our laps. We watched Two Broke Girls, like that. She moved her arm and when it touched mine I tensed up. I moved my arm and when it touched hers she smiled a little. She shifted herself about and she got herself comfortable, again. When she settled back down her shoulder was touching mine. I slid ahead on the seat and I turned around and I kissed her on the lips. She didn't kiss me back and I sat back around by her. But I slid back up on it and I kissed her on them, again. This time she kissed me back. She let me hug her, now, too. As I sat back around by her my hand brushed over her sweater where her boobs were. She didn't move away from me or stiffen up. So, I went back, and I put it back there. She tensed up and I took it back away. But I went back again, and I put it back there again. Now we sat there together and watched t v, like that. Now I reached around behind her. I pulled her sweater up over her head. I reached around behind her again. I unhooked her bra and I watched it fall down into her lap. Her bared tits stuck straight out. They didn't droop even a little bit. I helped her lay back onto the couch. I got in between her legs and I reached up in under her sweater to fondle her breast. But before I could do it her hands shot up and she stabbed me in the chest with her fingers. Stunned, I froze there, unable to move. It was a minute before I could even think, again. I finally got back off her. We both sat back up. We put our hands back into our laps. I didn't stay long, after that. She didn't sit back close to me, again. I felt awkward sitting there with her. I felt that I should probably go. I got back up careful not to show my feelings. I took a first step out to the door. She got up as though to come behind me. We walked out to it, me in front, her behind. We didn't kiss or hug, at it. We said goodbye, and I left. Neither of us called, again. I felt bad for going over there the way, that I did. I felt as bad that she would hit me so hard. But I guess that's what things came to. I never went back to see her, again. We haven't seen or talked to each other, since.

The End

ABOUT THE AUTHOR

Charles Forgrave lives in Sault Ste. Marie, Michigan. He was raised in Iroquois Beach, a nearby fishing and lumbering village. He and his wife, Linda, are raising two beautiful children, Trey and Tishella.

ABOUT THE BOOK

Set in Michigan's beautiful and remote Upper Peninsula on the shore of Lake Superior Love Buries a Spring Bird is a heart-breaking love story. Cortney and Jackie fall deeply and innocently in love in a lumbering and fishing village. Their relationship moves into the nearby town of Sault Ste. Marie where life's realities seep in and determines their future. Written in a prose style that is both fresh and vivid, the author's characters emote at a level seldom achieved in modern writing.

Made in the USA
Monee, IL
12 September 2022